Big Dogs
(Barking)

by Garrison Somers

Blotter Books

Somers, Garrison 1957 -
Big Dogs (Barking)
ISBN 979-8-9859878-2-9
Published in the United States by
Blotter Books
an imprint of The Blotter Magazine, Inc.
1010 Hale Street, Durham, NC 27705
Printed and bound in the USA

Big Dogs (Barking)

BY
GARRISON SOMERS

For Joe B. and Richard V. I. because they get it.

Big Dogs (Barking)

"Why don't we still got the 380?" mopes the rangy young man with the simple-syrup drawl, looking through the windshield at the world outside, but slumped down in his seat, his uniform shirt rumpling. "That 380 was all get up and go. No quit in it, I'll tell you that for nothing."

The simple, slumping, rumpling, grumpy fellow's name is, for reasons that we will not delve into, Waldo Ludlow. It is nearly a palindrome, a fact that has followed him through his young life. *Wall-dull Dud-lull* was the reason he did not go out for sports in high school.

His partner - a comparably tall but much more broad-shouldered fellow named Thomas Smith, who is fully aware of the wall-dullness of his own name - is driving slowly east, intentionally, so that the setting sun doesn't flare in their eyes, along the two-lane road that meanders along the northern edge of the medium-sized East Texas town in which the two men serve as police officers. No, they are not in a big block Chevy, but a much more sedate, deeply disappointing Ford black-and-white.

The driver gives no answer. Ludlow looks over. Smith is maybe a handful of years older than he is, but his face is smooth-shaven and relaxed, he has no receding hairline, beetling of brow nor frown-wrinkles, so that they look of an age. Ludlow doesn't say anything else, because he can tell that at this moment, Smith is *thinking*. Ludlow knows there is no point to further verbal exposition from experience; when the tall man thinks, he goes somewhere else. In fact, Smith appears almost dazed, like someone might in the second immediately after you socked them pretty hard on the jaw. Not that many folks would choose to sock Smith. He is, as mentioned earlier, a rather large individual, and puts a cotton broadcloth uniform shirt to the test in the upper arms and chest. Nor is he slow-witted, although it seems to require most of his cerebral bandwidth to drive and think. But don't let appearances fool you. Smith sits straight, both hands on the wheel, and his hat rests on the leatherette seat between them. His hair is only just slightly out of skew, displaced presumably by the hat itself. The hat is a modern summer-weight peaked policeman's cover, with the small silver-colored shield device in front above the mirror-polished black *corfram* bill. Still, it looks like an old Tooty-and-Muldoon cop-cap, a reference with which you may not be familiar, yet both Ludlow, the thin man, and Smith, the big one, are, despite not having grown up with classic old-school television.

"A 380...," Ludlow repeats, his wistful voice trailing off to a whisper, seeing the huge automobile engine in his mind's eye, wanting to drive – no, *ride* – it, watching it expanding beyond its Detroit sheet-metal confines, growing muscular legs and bursting through in roaring dinosaur splendor. He adores three things in life: the car, a job where he gets to carry a gun and imagining that he looks like someone famous. Someone badass. He rubs his upper lip with his thumb and forefinger, smoothing his nigh-on invisible thin blond mustache. Audie frickin' Murphy. Well, maybe not quite *famous* anymore, but certainly retro-badass. Then he suddenly suspects that he is talking to himself, because once again, when Smith thinks he doesn't pay attention to talking that goes on around him, and Ludlow just likes saying stuff out loud. So let's call it like it is: two men, used to each other's proclivities and peculiarities. That said, Ludlow nods at his partner; acknowledgement and apology all in one. There's folks that can be interrupted and folks that can't.

"We can no longer be trusted with such things," says Smith after a block or two of the tires thumping on the expansion joints of the concrete road, as if he only just that moment and not necessarily out of context overheard his partner's first words, or, more ominously, his last thought, "as riot guns, armor-piercing ammunition, body cameras, or highspeed chases. For example, in a vehicle with a 380 cubic inch V-8 engine. It is said by those whose opinions matter in this regard that we have a *track record* of humping the duck." He doesn't smile at the locally selected idiom that means about the same thing as the old army-airforce saw *screwing the pooch*, and he doesn't take his eyes off the road ahead of them.

"One can only hope," Smith continues in his not quite high-school vice-principal tone, "that by 'track record' the opinion-holders mean only that we have had accidents a bit too frequently, and not actual track *records*."

"Yeah," the thin man agrees, half-heartedly. Ludlow pretty much knows he's not as smart as his partner, but is convinced that he's not a fool, either. He clings to that. Truth is a difficult taskmaster. He is only reminiscing. He leaves off the conversing with, "I miss it, though."

Ludlow recollects when he met Smith, and how at first he thought the man was stiff and oddly quiet. A firm hand-shake, but he didn't offer his first name. When they were made partners, was it just random chance? Or was there something intentional in the assignment, two parts making something greater? In any case it wasn't long before the desk sergeant, an older fellow who might very well have been constructed at the same time as the desk, if not the police station itself, began calling them *Ludlow and Smith, those two nit-wits.* Just because, like tonight, they were on night-shift and made that one mistake. Well, actually, their *initial* mistake. Mistakes are fun for everyone except the poor slobs committing them, aren't they? And a nick-name will stick worse than bulldog cactus spines, particularly if you don't want it to, and often for no more reason than you went somewhere without looking around first. Ludlow knows better now. That is, he knows that Smith is smarter than he is. And a good partner. One that doesn't throw you under the bus to save his own reputation. That doesn't necessarily make the tall fellow a rocket scientist, not by any means. Just smarter than him.

Rocket science smart isn't a high priority, anyhow, here in Garrison, Tex-by-God-Ass. There are no NCIS procedu-rals, or Law & Order, or genius *squints* doing pathological anthropology or whatever other TV show bullcrap fits here - references that only superficially break into Ludlow's consciousness - just the occasional drunk swerving determinedly down Main or a blue-coif'd granny backing over a mailbox with her Oldsmobile and bursting into tears at the desk-sergeant because she's wrecked federal property. Weed-enhanced teenagers trying out *drifting* skills over in the Target parking lot. Or the kind of curious stuff that happens in a medium-small town where there aint much to do. Medicated crazies meditating on the side of the road. Scruffy little boys trying their shoplifting skills. Upstanding women members of the community catfighting outright in public with one another. Traffic-wounded armadillos chasing their perpetrators. Alien abductions. OK, then. He stands corrected. As the man might or might not have said, it takes all types of wackos to make a village.

What the Garrison PD wants – what they require, see – of their employees is to follow the rules, display polite and thoughtful behavior, and a fair bit of blindness to the quirky events, and certainly a zipped, nearly invisible blonde mustached lip doesn't hurt, neither.

The squad car rolls on through the dust and gravel as the cloud-clear sky rolls through the shades of blue towards darkness.

Earlier that afternoon:

On the biggest day of the year, bigger than Christmas and the A&M game and July Fourth rolled together, he made the decision to give up the Thunderbird. It was his pride and joy and the very idea of saying goodbye to it was choking-feeling, tear-bringing, hand-wringing and all such sad stuff that he could imagine if not actually experience. He was, after all, a heartless, nerveless and emotionless banker. Like his daddy before him: the elder Mr. Woodrow, currently an incontinent resident of These Contented United Suites –

also quietly referred to as Woodrow Senior, had run this place like it was a stout oaken sailing ship stoked with ripe breadfruit and he was a grumpy captain bound for London. The Thunderbird, a 1963 Landau, which as a youth Woodrow Junior indelibly yet mistakenly assumed was named after that actor who tried to shoot Cary Grant near the end of *North by Northwest*, had been his father's actual baby, the crown jewel of the firm, topic of conversation for anyone in town who saw it.

The elder Mr. Woodrow, back when he was a younger Man With A Bank, rode it slowly through the center of town to perform weekend errands or star in Independence Day parades as if it were a golden palomino stallion just a spur-jab from galloping off down the street, across town and into the Texas mesquite-range. There was never a soft-bottomed, smiling Miss Garrison perched with her feet on the seat, no paper sign dangling from the side of the T-Bird announcing its presence. The Bank never played second fiddle to star-spangled bosoms or fluttering red-white-and-blue bunting. Nosiree-Bob. No one needed to tell anyone in town that this was The Bank and that you should let The Bank handle all of your financial needs. The older man occasionally but not always permitted young Woodrow – just a boy in a yoke-front shirt with mother-of-pearl snaps and a straw hat – to sit in the front with him, so long as he did the waving without complaining about sore arms and didn't ask for a soda-pop or whine that he was hungry. When the Mexican shave-ice man offered Woodrow junior a frozen red-white-and-blue skyrocket popsicle, his father gave him such a look that the youngster never ate one again.

Parades! Oh, the joy and pride of being the absolute center of the universe.... The Thunderbird rumbling just far back enough from the high-school band and the flag-corps and the flaming-baton-twirling beauties to bask in the attention that the music and long legs and fire garnered, but not to be actually associated with any wool-blend uniformed sad-sacks with their cornets and clarinets. Once, as a hot-blooded male teenager, Woodrow had asked his father if he might drive the...baby.

No. You just want to...*misbehave* with some *trollop*. Well, hell yeah, he'd thought. Of course that's what I want to do! As a young man, Woodrow asked his father again if he could have the car.

No. You just want to show off. Someday? he'd followed-up. Woodrow Senior had slowly shaken his head. Then, as an elderly man, when Woodrow Senior was finally, inexorably relieved of responsibilities to the bank and the keys to the car, young Woodrow, no longer young himself, still didn't drive the damned thing. Just parked it in the garage, covered in protective canvas. Like a valuable painting by an old master that he didn't even like looking at.

And now this. *Incompetent*, his father had called him in a rare but recent moment of semi-lucidity. Followed by a rambling of sorts: there's only one central jewel in a crown, like the sun in the sky. You can't make chicken salad out of chicken shit. No one grows roses by moonlight. And you blew it, champ. It was slightly bewildering, but he got the gist of it all.

Young Mr. Woodrow - that is, the present Mr. Woodrow of The Bank - leaned back in the high-backed, light-brown cowhide chair. He let out a half groan, half belch. Combined complaint of the soul and stomach. *Ah, shit.*

"Scandal is the sorest shot," he vaguely paraphrased some poet or other. Rubbed his eyes under his thick thumbs until he saw geometric shapes and palette colors. Released them from the pressure and blinked back tears. "And denial is the darkest river." He was referring of course to the bank's connection with the oil and sex, family values and sex, money and sex *expose* that the local paper's publisher had unearthed and was going to reveal in print, in spite of Woodrow's stern talk – that it would spoil the event to have its chief sponsor dragged over the coals so. It might, he hinted, even ruin The Bank. The publisher, Patterson, had laughed, actually snorted in Mr. Woodrow's face. Ruin The Bank, or ruin you?

Me, of course. Ah, scandal. It used to have a set of rules that made sense. A playbook to follow. Nowadays, well, who had a remote clue what people would put up with and what would cause them to break out the pitchforks and torches? *That'll teach you, you fool*, he didn't say, but might as well have, because Woodrow left the paper's office with a pain behind his eyebrows and revenge on his mind.

"I'll get you," he mumbled at Patterson as the door incongruously clicked quietly shut.

"There are other sponsors," the publisher's parting *passant*.

"Ah...," Woodrow groaned again. "...shit."

He loosened his tie and unbuttoned his sleeves. What to do? He had no more notion of how to do damage control, rally the troops, circle the wagons nor exact revenge than he had of methods for flying to the moon. I am completely underprepared, he realized. Looking at his desk, he pushed things out of the way with the damp, flaccid flat of his palms. Pen and paper, set in preparation. A *courtesy* proof copy of the aforementioned story. A glossy color snap of the Thunderbird, propped in a Plexiglas frame. In it, he stood alone beside *the baby*, the automobile sparkling candy-apple red and the banker in his deepest, most sincerely blue suit. Texas Dust selecting to defy gravity's law by refusing to land on the car's brilliant paint and chrome. Woodrow son of Woodrow – his every shining and remaining hair perfect, face cracking under the phenomenal weight of a fairly scary looking smile.

Closing his eyes, he braced his chin on his forearms, curled his fingers around his face. Down here, in the dark of his own creation, Woodrow the Younger smelled the brimstone of his devil's deal.

Scandals happen every day, and...no one cares what the details are. Only that *they are*. And who is involved. And what damage it might cause. Let me see, and decide for myself, each of us thinks, if this automobile accident is horribly gruesome. If it is worthy of my consideration. Of continued attention. If it is, then we really don't care what the cause is, do we?

He had dragged – or more precisely was about to have dragged - down the name of his father's bank. Not so long ago, a local bank had power to bend will and control hope. A wise banker was the conscientious conscience of his town. All well and good for its time, no argument, something and someone had to be the foundation of the community. But in the age of fiber optics a fellow could take their *will* and *hope* to a bank in...Fargo if he wished, and no hard feelings, right?

Still, the Bank flourished, because many did not yet know such truths. It kept its name intact, for its name was neither necessarily a perfect good nor a flawed bad. Woodrow the younger had learned one thing well from his father, up there with the best glad-hand men in finance. Woodrow Senior had been the emperor of mumbling *aw, shucks'es* and "Well, son, that aint nothing but a thing" so that his customers got to calling him Woodrow Well, son; behind his back to be sure, but he knew about it and chuckled from the cowhide chair with a rumble like far off thunder. If folks are talking about you, but it doesn't kill you, you're doing well, Senior instructed Younger. So long as you don't mess on the company name, that is. The company name is all you've got, especially if folks observe that there are...alternate options. You can wrestle with time and destiny, but you can't deny dishonor. Woodrow had listened to his father from a customer chair across from the massive mahogany desk at which he now sat, nodding and chewing on a Cuban the size of an infant's forearm.

Don't mess on the company name. As simple a set of instructions as "do unto others..." And yet he seemed to have done precisely that. So maybe it required more specificity, after all. Like "don't dip you're your wick in the inkwell," or something to that effect. That made him think about *her* for a moment. *Stop drifting*, he thought. Then, damn - even the voice of angry chastisement was his father's. You imbecile!

Woodrow made a mental list. What now?

1) Recant all of my lies. Come clean in front of God and everyone. That thought floated up into thin, thin, thin air and popped with a distant, abrupt sound. The predictably soon-to-be-erstwhile banker ran his fingers through his thin thin *thin* hair. In his mind's ear he could hear the voice saying, "For Pete's sake, boy, get a grip." Once again, no further explanation. Just "get a grip." On the whole, advice of no use, all things considered.

2) Pay off everyone involved. A good oilman's response to problems. Good for everything from collapsing derricks and offshore rigs to the Kennedy assassination to drunken

tanker captains to cheating on government contracts for the past two decades. Money can't buy you love, old John Lennon would have said, but hell if it doesn't let you borrow love for a good while. Is there enough money? Of course, there's always enough money, so long as you aren't limited to using your own. He set this idea in a holding pattern over the runway.

3) And speaking of run: run, quick like a rabbit, quick as an east Texas jackrabbit in the limestone scrub. Fella, if you can't outgun, *outrun*.

Note: So far, Woodrow hated all of these so-called solutions. Hated, fiercely with a vengeance. His temples throbbed, either from the uncomfortable position that leaning over on his desk put him in, or the uncomfortable position that being part of an *indignity* put him in. Was there no one who could give him an actually good idea – something he could sink his teeth into?

4) Not particularly helpful but at least not a terrible idea: send out for a burger from the Joint. That rat-bastard Willard could make him a double-cheese with hot sauce and a Frito-pie. A Huffman's Black Cherry chilling on the side. Maybe a bowl of banana pudding, if there was any today. Woodrow knew that they don't make *'nanner puddin'* every day. Just why not, Woodrow couldn't imagine. Make the damned banana pudding, why don't you?

5) After consuming said burger, the poured into the bag chili, cheese and chip concoction called "Frito-pie," cold drink and pudding, take a short nap. There was a matching cowhide-covered couch in Woodrow's office. It was more for impressing customers rather than the occasional power-eye-shut, but he had used it from time to time for getting rid of headaches, literal rather than figurative. Today was looking

like a good day for it. With his stomach distended, he would snore like a ripsaw working through spruce logs.

6) After waking up, exact a plan for taking down the newspaper, lock stock and barrel, if not before they attempt to take down the Bank and him, then in certain retribution. Tee-hee. He liked the idea of destroying a unit of the fifth estate. After all, who didn't? The details, however, of such a happy event, eluded him. Ah, the devil was always in the details. So, saith the man, it goes...

The banker pushed all of those thoughts out of his way like wrapping paper around a Christmas tree, pressed a button on a machine on his desk and waited a fraction of a moment.

"Yes, sir," said a woman's voice. Without preamble, Woodrow listed foodstuffs, as if the woman understood automagically what on Earth he was talking about, then clicked off. She didn't, but familiar with Mr. Woodrow made some assumptions and reached some conclusions and rang up the Joint. The grill wasn't on yet, but she explained who was ordering and Willard got to work. It always cost Woodrow extra for this service, but he'd never know and who was hurt by that?

Meanwhile, Woodrow, his head thumping now to the beat of a big-band drum, actually cleared his whole iconic banker's landing-field of a desk of clutter, stuff, memorabilia, memoranda, crapdoodle, *chazerai*, ephemera, jetsam and other apparently useless extraneous shit in one fell swoop. Or, conversely, one swell *foop*, he thought without smiling. Tugged off his cufflinks and slang them to the carpet. Rolled up his sleeves – hard work coming! Yanked a piece of letterhead from his desk drawer, tore it, and pulled another more successfully. A pen, from the desk drawer, not the stupid three-hundred-dollar antique bakelite fountain pen he had just catapulted to the floor. Just a Bic. French company. One good thing from France. Surprising, considering. Or maybe not. They do a lot of capitulating and require reliable writing materials for surrender notes.

I surrender – he began, briefly giggling like a little girl. It worked for France, why not me? Scratched a line through it.

I'm not sorry, you bastards! he began again. *I didn't know that she was allergic to olive oil. Who's allergic to olive oil?* Other than Popeye the Sailor? Woodrow held in his mighty guffaw until hysterical tears squirted out from his eyes and he rubbed them with his hairy forearms rather than the silk pocket square from his jacket, currently draped behind him over the cowhide chair. He pulled himself together. Not all that funny, he scolded himself and shook all over like a speckled-puppy. Mirth became Woodrow, but no one peeped in through the keyhole to witness and validate his joy. He put another blue line through the words and crumpled the paper. Flicked it to the floor with a desktop-football kick that would have made any sixth-grade boy proud. Found a third sheet of letterhead and began more carefully scribbling his deviltry notes.

Sunset:

Officer Smith ponders the cosmic artistry that goes behind creation of a sunset. Mysterious chemistry from the closest star, conveniently producing a certain kind of light energy and disseminating it through the vapor manufactured of hydrogen and oxygen molecules, refracting...or is it reflecting, he can't at that moment say with certitude which. The visual event they're having at the moment is a doozy, though. It is unusually breathtaking. He turns the cruiser into the parking lot of a closed bakery. They used to make very fine donuts here, but the shop boxed it up for good during the last recession. Cracks in the parking lot are leaking overgrown tufts of gray weeds. When our things go away, and nothing replaces them, it is the definition of despair, he thinks. A picture of her comes to mind, but he shoves it back in its mental cubbyhole. Not the time for it, he tells himself.

Too damned bad, his brain replies aggressively. You are not the boss of me. No matter how he attempts to not think of her, it insistently places the image of her up on the current thoughts-easel again. Long hair, pulled back over her ears. She is smiling that smile of hers, the one that is and isn't a happy look. Like the painting in the Louvre properly entitled La Gioconda after a particular yet otherwise forgettable noblewoman of Tuscany. He stares out the window at the shirt-tail shreds of sunset, but is not really seeing it anymore. Her eyes are closed – he knows them, though, by heart. As one should. Her lips are thin but soft. She is shy about certain things – her cheeks are acne-scarred, her neck very short. Smith doesn't care, never has cared. If you like someone, want to make them yours and to give yourself to them, it doesn't matter what they think they look like. And if they like you as well, they can overcome your various and sundry flaws, too. Or, rather, that is the way it should be, but sometimes isn't. As Smith knows. And, like a sunset, not everything wonderful can be held in place by sheer force of will.

"How does a donut shop go out of business?" Ludlow asks softly; perhaps to him, perhaps only to himself. Smith, snapped back to the now, doesn't reply. It is a question only a skinny policeman can ask without recognizing the irony. He wants to tell his partner to look up at the sunset but

18

doesn't. Either it occurs to you to look at sunsets or you make comments about donuts.

Simple enough, Smith thinks. Bad business plan is all. He recalls with a small compression of his left eyebrow the absolute worst business plan of all time. A lunch kiosk, downtown – good traffic, easy to make the product. How hard is it to boil hotdogs and put them on a steamed bun? Annie Pepper was one of the classmates he'd attended high school with. Nice enough, a little bit dim to be sure, but what she lacked in so-called smarts she made up for with what people refer to as *isn't she sweet?* Even she couldn't mess up a hotdog stand. Then she named it. Painted herself a sign, and screwed it in, literally and figuratively as it turned out, to the front of the kiosk. *Anne's Franks.* Yeah, well, so there you go. It might have survived the current attitude towards humor, but not back then. Smith shook his head. Even in a simple little burg like Garrison, Tex-by-God-Ass, you can't make certain mistakes.

The alarm on Smith's watch trills. He taps a button to stifle the sound and takes one last glance out of the window. The oranges are gone, faded to campfire-coal maroons. He's not hungry, but if they don't go get their supper now, everything will be closed except for the fast-food crap out near the interstate.

"Mexican," Ludlow votes, without preamble. Smith nods. He wheels the cruiser around in the parking lot, dodging bits of more than one shattered pop bottle twinkling in the day's last light.

Evening:
Patterson sat. Considered himself: Why am I here? What sort of man am I? What are my good points and what

are my weaknesses? Who plots against me and which bastards are my true friends? What can be repaired and what is too far gone? Such are the simple questions a newspaper-man near the bitter end of the age of newsprint must ask himself, and anyone else who will listen. Ponder, ponder... Patterson nearly fell asleep, propped by pillows in the deep green cloth of his chair, thinking heavily on what made up the things that were uniquely him.

Words. Just words. Sad, he had to admit, that I even bore myself to exhaustion. Either that, or drive myself to dis-traction. But he could exorcise out no tears for himself, could not bring himself to a dry weep. I am not even worthy of a sniffle, he thought. And my sniffle is but a piffle.

Eventually, his introspection wound down. His eyes rolled to the black forest cuckoo marching in step on the wall above the gray television screen. The hands were invisible. Its bronze counterweights neared the top of the console. The room was shadowy and night displayed in each window. How long have I been sitting here? Forever? Whatever was I watching on TV? He couldn't recall. He reached down and took a sip of his coffee. It was cloyingly sweet and stone cold-dead-in-the-market.

After a while the cuckoo clucked at him once, providing no further insight as to the actual time of night. Somewhere in the house, his wife, Madolyn, slept: early to bed, early, etcetera. She would be gently, reliably snoring, like the purr of an old tomcat, Patterson knew, oblivious to his pain, or rather, to his inability to produce pain within himself.

His was the utter perfection of the catalog purchase called bland. No. Worse, that imperfection which blandness implied and unerringly delivered. He furrowed his brow, a single line of furry brown across his under-muscled forehead.

He held his face there for as long as he was able, a handful of tick-tocks of the weighted-wood pendulum, then released it. Ergs of work performed with no measurable result.

You know what? His left hand was tingling. It was almost indistinguishable, but there it was, nevertheless. Tingling, like it was going to sleep from lack of blood flow, or the pinching of a nerve in his elbow or wrist. Anticipated Acute Myocardial Infarction. Heart-fart. He imagined he felt his body failing, ineffably, inexorably. His hair ached. His eyes itched. Damnable, he thought. His time was shorter with each bippity-bam of his heart. How long did he have? How long? What could he accomplish worthy of a man in that time?

Because he had experienced trying to work without sleeping, he began to make his way in that direction. Stopped in the bathroom to try and pee. It always felt like his life force was draining from him, as he stood there with his vague little pecker in his hands. He shuddered, then sighed, a dribbly stream, the leaky drip finishing its coursing through the labyrinthine gutters and drains of his personal piping. Waste. If piss is my life force, then my pathetic existence was long since past zenith, and now steeply wanes.

"Enough," he said out loud to no one, then clamped his mouth shut. He didn't need his wife waking up and asking him *what are you doing? Is everything alright? Aren't you ever coming to bed?* Patterson padded to the bedroom without flushing, the tart bouquet of his own personal effluent lingering in his nostrils.

He gently sat on the edge of the bed. The television had been left on, flickering, volume turned down low. Madolyn's dreams, reported to him over morning coffee, were often of the quiet, panicky variety of close-to-death situation-tragedy that those more advanced in age tended to suffer. Tonight they must also include violent electric storms in the vacuum of space, sung to the tune of the talk-show host's nasal baritone. The ceiling fan above the queen mattress threw down warm air and the room felt dusty to him and inordinately small. Almost as if the walls were built with timers set, creeping in on silent motors to crush them while they snoozed.

He searched for the channel-changer in the litter of sheets and blanket. It skittered ahead of his fingers and then relented. Pressing the volume down to zero, he pointed it like a weapon at the screen. Crap, crap. Oh. No. Crappity-crap, paid-programming crap, broadcast news-crap, pay per crap, Home Box Crap. He settled on some thirteen minutes into An American In Paris, turned the sound up a careful notch, hummed *Give Me Songs By Shhhtraussss*, as Gene Kelly minced across the nineteen inch diagonal café wearing a dish-towel wrapped around his noggin. Once upon a time, he and Madolyn had been to Paris. Long, long ago. Small cups of coffee and standing in line to see paintings. Be damned if he ever went there again, anyway. You couldn't visit the Sacre Coeur, he'd once read online, without losing your wallet. They're all kids, the pickpockets, like rats they plague the tourist traps. Trudge up the overlook to the cathedral, they're there to sell you bottled water from little tables on the sidewalk. So you pull out a buck or two from your wallet, and now they know where your wallet is. It's all rehearsed and choreographed. - a little herd of them, the youngest ones Oliver Twist urchins, laughing and shouting and playing grab-ass around you bumping into you and innocently waving tourist brochures in your face while you laugh *non, non, merci,* and suddenly your wallet goes bye-bye.

Hold on a *merde*-ing minute, interrupted Gay Paree.

You're nothing to write home about, either, fella. Just another lumpy American with a complaining wife who doesn't like eating baked chicken dinner in the shank of the evening. For all of our sakes, don't bother booking a non-refundable flight or searching for accommodations in the *arrondisement* containing le Tour Eiffel, if you please.

Mon dieu, Paris was right! Of course, Patterson wasn't the same person he'd been back...then. The noticeable differences now being, ah, forget it. A laundry list. His patience, faded. His belly – inundated. His hair – immolated. His teeth – darkly shaded. A shortness to each breath, the foulness of each breath, the questionable regularity of each breath. His life was a TV ad for the medication cliché-a-thon.

Enough. Patterson pressed a button in the dark at random, because he didn't have the home position of the channel changer in his clicker hand. It must have been some sort of memory key-button, a home-free-all command perhaps, because suddenly it was the Travolta and brunette bang'd Thurman scene at the burger place, just prior to their dancing together. Ah-ha, thought Patterson. We've run the gamut. Gene Kelly to Vinny Vega. Some cultures never make this transition, from prurience to madness, but here we are, full circle, back to a childish insanity. He puffed through his nose, blinking at the flickering screen, through the Uma overdose, finally killed the pixilation with a lucky thumb depression. The TV set cooled with a sound like rats scuttering deeper into a torn burlap sack of rice.

And speaking of depression, Patterson shook his head, *aint we got fun?* His head wobbled badly on his shoulders, neck no longer performing well its prime function. The room pushed and pressed in around him. The soil of himself: his own skin sloughing off, his dandruff, his scuffings on the carpet, his tracking in of the dry grit of Texas, all clouding up around him. Scuttering and sloughing and scuffing – oh, my! Stealing each inhale-exhale combo, making the very air fetid. It was entirely too much. No rest for you! He stood, looked once more at Madolyn in her deep REM sleep, and padded out to the living room again. The curtains were open, because he had nothing to hide, nothing to keep private from prying eyes. When he was gone, soon, he, too, would leave a popping noise where air snapped in to fill the void, and the sputtering of retreating rats. Let us follow his dreary gaze: a wall with a print on it, something conventional, something bland, something with no intrinsic or esthetic value or taste. Nothing he liked, even. My dear, you've no sense of taste, Madolyn had said to him back when they still really talked to each other and so got all of the truth out as quickly as they could.

But there was also nothing there for which he might have eventually with time gained an affection. No photographs of family or friends or places he'd been or wished to go. No awards, awkward happy-snaps with co-workers, nary a portrait of beloved ancestors. No sense of the past, either, he told himself. Paint color? Named for something valuable – ivory? Pearl? A complete lie. Was there such a color called blandishment? Not even bland. Just blah. Everything was gray in the dark. He scratched his head. His world couldn't be more telling if he had been looking in a mirror. His clock was unwatchable, his life dark and dank.

That's what you get, said voice in his head. You are the voice of truth in a world that doesn't believe in truth – as if truth had become part of a belief system. Truth is a taskmaster that drives you fulltime, and then lets you fall by the wayside. Truth is a lover, and a hater. No one is happy with truth. And you're about to pull out the true keystone and let a whole lot of stuff fall.

It's my job.

Oh come now. That's just *crapinstance*. You don't have to do everything just because it's your job. You're doing this because you...enjoy it. And yet you constantly wash your hands of it, Pontius Macbeth.

Scuffing into the kitchen, he opened a high cabinet and drew down a small pint bottle of something liquid-ish called Rum Chata. Cranked the lid off and tilted without giving it a test-sniff. Sweet and hot. Cough! Strange stuff, must be something Madolyn bought for baking? He took another gulp and wandered back through the house. Felt the zing through the top of his head. Rum. Chatter.

Twisting the knob, out the front door he went. Stood on his stoop in his white undershirt and boxer shorts, crusty bare feet feeling the cool wet slate of the front walkway.

The night was close and still, heavily moist with falling dew. The humidity brushed at his face so thickly that he raised one hand to try and swipe it away. Above his head, stars pushing down their light, through the hubbub of electric clutter that people deployed against the gremlins that populated their thoughts of dark.

Night is why we invented religion. A desperate, endless quest for a cure for fear of the dark. Fear of the forever darkness we imagine death to be. Patterson knew only too well that incandescence cannot not fight off the monsters. The beast finds insidious methods of piercing the barriers people create to protect themselves.

Huffing deeply the dark air. Much better than the trapped space of his home, smelling of the transpiration of trees and tiny droplets of pollen although perfumed with the retrograde fallout from all things man, electric and petroleum, concrete and plastic. That it might be poison didn't trouble him. Patterson knew he was in the age-ballpark of done, whether or not the game was complete, the score tallied. No more was expected to come from him, no greatness, and so nothing would be lost by a foreshortening. He had no plans, and only the foggiest of goals.

Patterson shook his head again, stopped, listened for the tell-tale rattle of loose marbles. What is the *story* with all of this gloom? he chided himself Let's cut that out right now. He decided on the spur of the moment to knock it off. A midnight oasis of resolve. Anger, not frustration, if needs be. But no more of this woe towards me. Start a clean page in the journal.

Old habits die hard. Some men can't put paid to unfinished business. They investigate. Patterson was...designed to ask questions of others. Built – cobbled together, if necessary - to seek the truth, even when no one wanted it, preferring their own biases, wanting no more information beyond tribal recognition. You can't change the hardwiring, he told himself. Seven-year locusts chirred in the distance, their song reminiscent of nascent Messerschmitts diving on unsuspecting Basques. Seven years ago, they'd taken to hiding in the dirt beneath our feet, trusting in our administrative incompetence not to find them as they sleep, confident in our insolvency not to build castles over them. Here they were this summer, singing their shrill song and then finding a loved one. Back into the ground by Labor Day. Patterson frowned - I will never hear these particular, peculiarly loquacious creatures again. What will I be, seven years hence? Will my own fall come, hip snap, nine one one and a gurney ride? Have I provided for Madolyn in my own loss, or does she suffer through my lack? Perhaps her own sleeping permits some toxin to enter past weakened defenses, beginning her very own undoing? Oh, to be uncaring, like the locust, one short hectic season of life and love and then long soft sleep.

His wife's front garden. Hosta, leaves in various shades of gray rimmed with darker scales lining the slate walk down to the driveway, glared back at him. Oh yeah? he thought. He unzipped his fly and relieved himself some more of that evening's coffee, two fingers of scotch, some of the rumchatter and anything else that chose that route to abandon its host. Into the garden with you. Keeping the damned deer away. Patterson cared not a whit that some neighbor with a sleep disorder might choose at that very moment to glance past their curtains only to see him dangling his gristly, grizzly old pecker through the gap of his boxers, soaking the flowers. Shake, shake.

He held his hands to his chest, his soft, flabby chest, soft as if there were no ribs beneath his fingers, melted under the heat of his heart and blood and bile, and only the wax of fat and flesh held his private mulch and the compost of age inside. And that was when Patterson groaned aloud and began walking. His bare feet and tightening calves led him right out of one neighborhood and into another.

Dinner break:

The Mexican place is redolent with the sweet smoke and steam that pours off of *fajitas*, presented sizzling to the table in cast-iron pan and wafts up nostrils and clings to clothes. The tables' dark, dark wood is shiny from years of elbows leaning on them and hands wiping them clean after each meal served. It is a happy place, but joy is not forced, nothing false and silly; this time of evening the music is muted, and the walls entertained with framed black and white photos of...someplace. Mystery buildings, strangers smiling as they meet beneath trees, sunny summer mornings where hand-me-down bicycles lie strewn in front yards so one can almost hear the laughter of children playing two-deck *Slap* on living room floors, the mechanical whir of a reel-mower shaping a back-lawn. Smith and Ludlow have informed Dispatch that they are here, taking their evening meal. Dispatch has relayed the message to the town's other cruiser – the older fellow Keifer it is – that this is so, and he has acknowledged that he has the ball. They are, for the moment, off-duty.

Sitting by the cash register at a table near the entrance is a young woman with a clean, plain face, her dark hair pulled back in a loose pony. She greets the officers with professional familiarity and invites them to pick a table – the restaurant is quite empty because it is late, of course. She knows them. They know her. They sit at the table in the middle of the room, which seems an odd choice, but there you are. The young woman – her name may or may not be Serena; in all the times they've come here she has never actually introduced herself but wears a plastic tag with that name on it – comes immediately over to them after bookmarking a text she is reading and pours water into short juice glasses, takes drink orders which she already knows by heart (Coke with no ice and sweet tea, interchangeably, as whatever Smith orders, Ludlow picks the other, for reasons that Smith has never been interested enough in to ask and Ludlow has never revealed) and quickly returns with them, so that she can get the food order in so that the kitchen can close thereafter. She likes to talk, likes to smile at the policemen, and ask how their day is going – it always intrigues her that the end of her day is near and theirs is only just beginning. Ludlow does all of the talking for the two of them, but Smith knows all this about her because she has offered these particular details about herself: that she lives at home and works full time and takes classes at the community college three towns over and is worried about the mileage on her car, and he also knows it's nearly nine o'clock and she still lives at home and after she leaves for the evening she has to study before her mama will let her watch just one of her recorded stories before bedtime. What Smith is not aware of is that the class she currently takes is called *Infection Mitigation and Control in the Operating Theater*, although if he stood he could see the cover of the volume. Serena, for it is indeed her name, wants to be a nurse – no it is more than a *want*, but a *drive*, and she reads her textbooks whenever there is nothing else to be done, wherever there is sufficient light, which at this time of day is the host and cashier table near the front door, because the door has a large frosted window and it illuminates that part of the room well enough. She stops reading when the sun goes down, so Smith has never seen that or any other book, which is always stuffed in Serena's handbag tucked under the desk by the time the two policemen finish their meals. No one has to tell her even once that grades are the be-all and end-all in the mountain climb that is education.

Serena places two buckslips for orders of *picadillo chimichanga*, with beans, lettuce and red rice on the kitchen window shelf. The sizzle of the grill in the kitchen says done and done.

Sipping his Coke through a straw, Ludlow is like a fire-hose desperately pulling from a hydrant. Whew! The carbonated sugar bangs into his system like a bull-buffalo, horns and all. He actually feels his nervous system jump a handful of notches and his brain shifts gears. Imagine, he muses, what people smoking crack feel. Jeez, it must come damn close to lighting their heads on fire.

Now he wants to talk but looks at Smith and sees the tall man's impressively impassive demeanor and can't quite figure out how to...engage. They've been partners on the beat, if you can call it that, for three years now. And they've had their own fair share of...interesting moments. Why, he wonders, can't they be sociable, one with the other? Not friends, no; that would be asking a lot of someone like Smith. Ludlow expects that his partner doesn't have friends, even though he grew up here in town, and lives in his late mother's modest white clapboard house, set back from the street and with an actual flower garden out front. Ludlow, on another hand, is originally *from over to Tyler* as such things are said – and has a converted garage apartment here, and still drives for home cooking on weekends. Why can't they hang out at the end of a shift – get a sixpack and sit on camp chairs in the driveway before the sun gets too high and hot? Play a little penny-ante? Watch a game on TV – it doesn't even matter which. But the big man plays his cards pretty close to the vest. Ludlow wonders who tends the flowers. He just can't see Smith in shorts and a tee shirt kneeling on the ground pulling weeds. Still, maybe, they could talk from time to time, just jaw about stuff, and they both might benefit from it.

Right? Right, he silently answers himself.

Ahem. Without talking about that night. That's for sure. The night they fouled up. Humped the duck. And it was his fault. Well, probably, it was. No. take your medicine. His fault.

Big Dogs (Barking)

What then? What other subject is good enough for them to talk about, worthy to interrupt the recorded whisper of harmonious trumpets and deeply soulful Spanish guitars?

Ludlow's got nothing. His brain – well, there are days when he isn't actually sure it's even there anymore. What is his intellectual history? Got through high school by the skin of his teeth and joined the Texas Air Guard and they helped him with community college at night - kind of like Serena you know? - and he has an associate's degree in Criminal Justice, but recently he isn't confident that his mind's gears aren't stripped. He never did any drugs, and he only likes a beer or two on Saturday afternoons watching the 'horns play on his little wall-hung flat-screen, so he can't blame that for this tid-bit of an earlier-than-midlife crisis. One fact: he has no further aspirations. What can he do? What does he do well? Anything? What interests him? He actually turns that thought over and around for a moment, like a toddler checking out all of the sides of a wooden block just before throwing it at Mom's head. Shit, I thought aspiration was when you mistakenly get something caught in your wind-pipe.

He sighs loudly, leans back in his chair hoping against hope that Smith will just notice and start talking: *Don't be a jerk. Ask me a question, he silently begs. Anything! Ask me if I think our waitress is right pretty. Yeah, I do, buddy. Not really, but nice enough and you like her, so you should go say hey. Or even, he admits, let's talk about that night. Shit. Let's rehash it then. Go on!*

Smith glances over at Ludlow nearly squirming with discomfort in their silence. He wishes he could oblige his partner. He hears the sigh, like a well-trained beagle's when it wants to bark, to chase after squirrels or cats. But he sits there, stolid. This is a small town, he thinks. He wishes that

31

it wasn't. Was the right size for someone to learn through trial and error. He wishes he could tell Ludlow *partner, you should be looking for jobs somewhere else. This place is painted over for us.* Or was OK for him to go over to that woman with the long hair and say, how about we go get a cup of coffee? Better yet, we could one time maybe drive out and watch the sun go down. I like a good sunset, don't you? Yeah, I know you have a job and school and you're busy and don't know me, not really. It couldn't hurt to...

But that's not true. The world is a patchwork quilt made of infinitesimally small pieces - some sewn together tightly and others with chaotic looseness and lackadaisicality. He can't talk to Serena, or whatever she's actually named. Oh, the number of things he can't do. He can't even talk to his own partner. He can't tell Ludlow how to run his life, fix his life, make his life something better. Where are you going to go, son? What are you going to do? Well, get on it, then....

Finally, it seems that Ludlow surrenders, turns towards the kitchen door, and like a good puppy waits for supper to emerge. Smith relaxes one notch. It doesn't help.

Entre-acte:
**In which Keifer has an interaction with Billy,
not necessarily the night of our drama, but quite possibly.**
Kiefer had to content himself with the belief that he performed questionably useful acts. Driving what he still called a squad car around the darkened streets - Garrison was a tranquil place, sort of - it being July, the hum of AC challenged the supremacy of crickets and locusts. He was bored but didn't permit himself to switch on the radio and hunt down that Dallas C&W station, or some evangelical preach-

ing broadcasting out of Kilgore. Cruising slowly - no rush - looking at everything in its place. Lights were out where they should be; cars were parked. He rubbed his eyes to rid them of sleep's onset. *A cop pays attention, even in tranquility.*

His own squad car was old, with a single pimple on top and a hand-control spotlight where the left mirror would have been. The vehicle had cloth seats – who could imagine them in a modern police car - and it occasionally smelled. Only once had anyone ever thrown up back there, a long time ago, a member of a wedding party at the Elks, and that had been a command performance – Hey, fella, how 'bout can I give you a ride home? The shrimp cocktail, ginger-ale, scotch and champagne inside the rider returned with a vengeance to haunt them all. The rider (on duty Keifer never thought of people by their names, just riders and callers – he had to live here, too, and they might be neighbors and over the years he'd found it easier this way) had tried to catch the spew in his jacket pocket and then his cupped hands. Volume overcame capacity and the squad car suddenly needed detailing. The fella'd been apologetic – what else could he have done? - but on humid nights like tonight it smelled like a couch in a fraternity house. Keifer gnawed a stick of Black-Jack gum, its licorice flavor offsetting the aroma. The downtown CVS kept a small stock of the little blue packs special for him. He smiled at that. It's what you used to do when you wanted *Po-Lease* protection, ostensibly from little old ladies gossiping in the analgesic aisle. Not that such was necessary; all they had to do was ask and he'd make the drive-by and break up the traffic. Still, it was nice to see that some things, some, mind you, were still around. Like him and this squad car. He liked old things and old ways.

He parked behind the big plywood sign for the Sno-Ball

shack that sold sickly sweet cones from May through October on the future Wal-Mart parking lot. This was a good spot for nabbing the occasional stranger that cut through town to get to the Shreveport expressway and neglected to sit through the traffic light cycle that was on all night. Yeah, it was kind of dumb both to run a red light and to have it cycling even when there was no cross traffic. But that was another of the old things whose passing he would regret when the town's fathers finally paid for time-and-traffic sensors. And, sure, he felt kind of pointless sitting in the dark trying to anticipate a scofflaw, but that was what the job entailed. Keifer never wished for more action, as a younger man might have. He didn't want anything more than was already here. Nobody teased him about it back at the station, there was something about Keifer that didn't permit razzing, although he'd never said anything regarding such behavior. He had a way that just nipped it off beforehand, like he was someone that should be left alone.

His first sandwich would come at two AM. The other was his breakfast reward. If he ate both at two, he would go into "a food-coma", as the teens in his church congregation youth-group called it. And steering around in a squad car wasn't enough exercise to burn off two pulled-pork sand-wiches. Keifer recognized the signs – he couldn't fit in the same sized uniform he'd worn a couple of years back. His workhorse thermos was a three-cupper; half hi-test, half decaf, because all of that fully caffeinated would give him what the same batch of kids referred to as "the zooms".

The police scanner was quiet. He'd rigged it to pick up the emergency weather band as well, gleaning information from the NWS on thunder-boomers and twisters, especially when it pertained to Gregg County. Once upon a time you had to keep your windows open and keep tasting the air, for rain and dust and that ineffable tang a tornado had. Without that sense, folks had been lost to the tornadoes that dropped from thunderheads unexpectedly (back when it was almost all unexpected, before the advent of Doppler radar and storm advisories and satellite photography), whisking homes into the never-never and snatching lives with caprice. And the weather report was just more interesting than listening to the white noise of the local scanner, with only the occasional blip of chatter from out of town when police frequencies bent in the humid air. Tonight, though, even the sky was asleep.

At the far end of his patrol, Keifer drove past The Joint. Four hours after locking up, the air around the place still smelled like Willard had just burned the last burger to a crisp, his own late supper before scraping the grill and going home to watch Tennessee Walker training on Rural Farm TV. Like Keifer, there were other solitary folks with patterns to their lives, habits and personal proclivities. Out beyond The Joint was the great empty road, extending to other worlds - maybe towns like this, and maybe just a bit different. He had coveted, reached and passed that day when he should have kept on driving - if there'd been something out there, he had felt its pull but hadn't responded. Now, that pull wasn't there anymore. Or maybe he couldn't tell, his guts occasionally twisted for something but he suspected they would never again have that strange attraction for the unknown, or someone to share it with. He crunched the squad car around in The Joint's gravel parking lot and cruised deliberately back towards town.

Two o'clock came and went. He munched his sandwich and eyed the other one thoughtfully, sipping warm coffee.

The radio's static calmed him like a mother's hushing whisper on another normal, quiet night. Keifer felt something though, anticipation, at the tip of his tongue, like tasting the rising wind for forthcoming rain. It sent a tingle along his spine, from his backside to the roots of his hair.

"Disturbance call, sergeant, pick up," a somnolent voice broke into his thoughts. It sounded like Desk was as subtly entranced by this dog-watch hour as he was.

"Here," he said. Thank the Lord the staff ignored all radio bullshit; it was irritating to try and maintain what might have been thought of as proper police jargon etiquette. It was much simpler just to talk, and if privacy was needed to use a land-line telephone. Technology, and everyone's access to it, had nearly driven them back to the days of call-boxes.

"Mrs. Dunwood called in. Someone is messing with her goats," said the 'Desk Sergeant,' a young woman named Clara who worked in the mayor's office and did the occasional night shift as a dispatch. Keifer winced. He had a passing familiarity with Mrs. Dunwood. She owned a small farm on the outskirts. Not even really a farm, sort of a once-was-a-farm. He saw her occasionally at First Baptist; she too sat in the back although he'd never passed the peace with her. The geese in the fellowship hall, those front-pew ladies that found the venue of Christian brotherhood a perfect opportunity to talk about other people's problems, surely had words about her broken marriage and strange behaviors.

"Messing?" Keifer said. He could imagine boys from the high school pestering the animals. Way back as a teen he had done this thing with his friends called Cow Tipping, which involved high-school athletes slamming full steam into the sides of Herefords, t-boning them, as it were. Sort of football training meets large animal husbandry. It turned out that although some cows sleep standing up, the truth was that cattle preferred to lie down to sleep. And in the dark it was difficult to tell the difference between a standing and sleeping cow and a merely resting cow, not to mention that pertinent difference between a cow and a bull. When you charged a merely resting bull, the tables became swiftly turned against you. Keifer had only cow tipped the one time before he became bored with such bovine hi-jinks.

"She didn't clarify, Sergeant," Clara said. "She did say she's called before about this."

Keifer closed his eyes. It hadn't been his call before - Ludlow or Smith, maybe; those nitwits.

"She asked if you would call in and I would connect you with her." Desk referred to the aforementioned land-line procedure. He was back at the junction that offered the Wal-Mart construction site or down-town. He took the Wal-Mart turn. There was an old phone stall in front of the dry-cleaners which had sold out to the big store developers, leaving everyone in town the option to either buy wash-and-wear or mail their clothes to Tyler. The phone hadn't been disconnected yet because the guys working on the Wal-Mart liked to get take-out Mexican. Keifer rolled through the parking lot, past the Sno-Ball stand and up onto the bulldozer-crushed macadam at the construction site.

He picked around in his ashtray for change. Crap. He'd have to dial collect. Keifer smiled at the looniness of dialing collect across town on a police call.

"Clara, accept the charges, for crying out loud," Keifer quickly said, as the automated operator offered Desk the option to take his call. He shushed her when she asked what had happened, and told her to dial Mrs. Dunwood. There was a clicking in his ear as the call rang through.

"Hello?"

"Mrs. Dunwood?" Keifer started. "This is Sergeant Keifer with the police department. Good evening. You called in a complaint?"

"No," Mrs. Dunwood said. Keifer felt his eyebrows go up. The woman's voice was low and clear. She was wide awake. "It is most certainly not a good evening. I'm trying to report an attack."

"An attack," Keifer said. A while back he had taken a class in Dallas on improving police listening skills. Repeating back key elements of a conversation showed interest.

"You need to come here," the woman said. It wasn't a request. A frown crossed Keifer's face.

"Yes, ma'am. I'll be there in ten minutes," he said and hung up. He'd found there were times when it just paid to do what you were told.

Not another vehicle passed him on the roads over to Mrs. Dunwood's farm. The only sound was his car and the rush of cool air through the window past his ears.

Mrs. Dunwood stood outside her clapboard bungalow, looking like a statue in the front yard. Keifer stepped from his car, his small flashlight in hand. He left it off, as he saw Mrs. Dunwood was wearing a nightgown. She was a deeply unpleasant-looking woman, the policeman thought, and the dark didn't help. Her voice was sharp-edged; despite her attempts to whisper, she couldn't.

"I've called about this before, Sergeant," Mrs. Dunwood spat.

"Yes ma'am. But it was not immediately brought to my attention. All I know was what I have read on the call report," Keifer responded politely. He'd learned at a young age that it paid to be calm, particularly if your point could be seen as argumentative.

"Nobody likes me," the woman continued. She was lit from behind by a lamp in her house, diffused behind pulled curtains. Her hair stuck out on three points of the compass. "They act like I'm making crank calls."

"No, ma'am, I'm certain that's not the case," Keifer said. He was quite sure that this was the case, but in some situations he had found that gentle lies were preferable to belaboring the obvious. "Perhaps if you would explain to me what the problem is."

She sighed loudly at him, but he was relieved when without further prompting she began to explain.

Mrs. Dunwood raised animals for a petting zoo. There was no market for a petting zoo in Garrison, so the animals actually traveled with a carnival that cycled through Arklatex, that is, east Texas, western Louisiana, and the southwestern-most bit of Arkansas. They were unable to break into the Oklahoma county carnival market, for reasons that passed understanding to Mrs. Dunwood; the laws on transporting small-hoofed animals across state lines held no particular interest for her. On the aforementioned call, according to a report filed a number of months ago by one of Keifer's brother officers, she had claimed to have prowlers in her yard. They sought to take and hurt her animals. That, she said, is what she'd already told the police.

"I told them there was foul play afoot, and they just smiled at me, like I was simple minded," she told him. "They didn't take me seriously."

With Herculean effort, Keifer wrestled back a smile at the words *foul play afoot*. He pictured Mrs. Dunwood in bright daylight, in her nightgown. The thought killed his smile as dead as the last unicorn.

"I take you very seriously, Mrs. Dunwood," he assured her, trying to look her in the eye.

"You took your own time getting here," she sulked, but her face appeared to soften in the what Keifer now realized was moonlight.

"I was on the other side of town when the call came in," he said. "Why don't you tell me what's going on tonight." But Mrs. Dunwood must have sensed that she had center stage and wasn't going to give it up easily.

"You know, it's only because my husband's gone and I live alone that people bother me," she said. "Even the Pastor doesn't make visits." Mr. Dunwood was, indeed, gone. Keifer did not care to know why - that wasn't how he sorted and filed information about people - but he'd heard that a while back the couple had split, the old man taking their car and driving out of town, somewhere, away. Well, that was how things sometimes went, Keifer supposed. They had no children. She was not, he guessed, in a position to hunt for another man, or even another car, although the police officer had a sudden vision of her, face painted blue, hair bound in a nest above her head in twine and small bones, a home-made crossbow in her hands, waiting patiently for two-legged prey of some ilk, or fighting off Roman legionaires invading her homeland.

Mrs. Dunwood shook her head and the wild mane of hair made a sad sound, like dry hay in a breeze. No, Keifer admitted, that was an out-and-out lie. Her hair only seemed like straw. She pointed her finger accusatorily at Keifer. He reminded himself as well that she only seemed like a pos-sessed demon in the night. "I'm sick of it, too. And I want it to stop." He thought he felt her spittle on his cheeks with the word *Stop*.

"And do you know what they do? They mess with the animals. Who messes with animals, Officer?" He was going to remind her that he was a police sergeant, but she held up her hands in front of him, too closely. They had the coppery stink of blood. Blood...and something else.

"What is that?" Keifer asked the grim-faced woman. She grimaced, furious with him.

"Someone attacked my goat!" she said curtly. Even in the dark, her look said *laugh and ye shall regret.* He took the unspoken, arcane advice to heart.

Mrs. Dunwood turned and started towards the back of her bungalow. Keifer felt obliged to follow.

The night air chose that moment to reach dew point. Moonlit mist rose around their feet theatrically. In her nightgown, Mrs. Dunwood looked exceedingly witchlike, seeming to float across the ground without walking. Trailing behind her, Keifer felt ill for some reason. The police officer resisted the urge to turn on his flashlight, suddenly fearful in some childish place in his mind that this event would turn into a nightmare. He tucked it in his belt.

"Mostly, I just want to be left alone, you know," Mrs. Dunwood stopped near the fence in her back yard that separated the part where she ran the lawn mower from the part where she raised her animals. She turned back to face Keifer. "Even out here, no one respects that. They imagine they're all wonderful, loveable folks, with goodness in their hearts." She tried to push her hair down with one bloodstained hand, but it wasn't having any of it, and was witchier than before.

"Yes, ma'am," Keifer said. He smelled barnyard now, but not terrible. She appeared to keep the place as clean as such things could be kept, mucking out enclosures and putting a layer of hay on the manure pile every now and then to tamp down the aroma and aid in the composting. As if reading his mind, Mrs. Dunwood sniffed deeply.

"I sell the litter to the colored gentlemen for putting in gardens," she said, referring to the two old men with their manure truck. "That and the petting zoo's orders keep me in bread and water. My old man was as useless a piece of baggage as ever there was one. Didn't like working the moment he quit school. How do you become an adult without understanding that you're gonna have to do something worthwhile in order to feed yourself."

Keifer shrugged unprofessionally. He knew it was some folks' nature that made them lazy. Like water, they would always seek their lowest level.

"But then to piss and moan about the turns that life had taken?" Mrs. Dunwood continued. "Didn't make sense to me. He was as lazy as a dry stick and was the world's worst complainer. You can't have it both ways, can you?"

"No, ma'am," Keifer said quietly. "I suppose you can't."

"So he's gone, and good riddance. And of course he took the Ford. I'm not complaining about that. I like walking and I like working, and I don't shy away from the dirt, like some do. There's women go their whole lives without getting a grain of sand under their fingernails. Can't stand the pong of their own farts." Her head cocked to one side, she crossed her arms. "But them bitches at church blame me for it. For him leaving. For being in the situation I'm in. Go figure."

Keifer stood still. What else was there to say? His listening skills class said that there was nothing wrong with the occasional silence. He believed whole-heartedly in that old chestnut 'best keep your mouth shut and seem stupid than open it and remove all doubt'.

"Well," Mrs. Dunwood said, staring through the dimness yet somehow seeing him. "You aint much to look at, and you sure don't talk."

Keifer's eyebrows went up.

"I'm sorry?" he said.

"What are you good for?" she asked. He could detect the snide in her voice, but let it go. It was almost like she was talking to herself as much as him.

"Ma'am. I'm just trying to help," he said. "You said you had an attack."

'He hurt my goat," she said, back on task and quietly furious again.

"Who did?" Keifer asked.

"That goat was just a yearling," she said, ignoring his question. She pressed her hair down again and this time it stayed, framing her face, as if the moisture in the air wasn't fighting it anymore. While earlier she had looked frightful, now she was not so. "There's something wrong if you don't like animals, but there's some like that. I guess I can't hold fault. But it's another thing altogether if you feel you gotta go out and hurt them, just to do such a thing."

"What happened, Mrs. Dunwood?" Keifer pressed. As she had before, the woman seemed calmed at the sound of her own name.

"I didn't call earlier, on account of those others didn't pay attention like you do," she said.

"Others?"

"Them younger policemen."

Ah, he thought. Those two nit-wits, Smith and Ludlow.

"They're maybe just playing at police," she said tangentially. "Or too young. Gotta teach them where to take a crap and where not. They're just happy to be wearing a uniform over their skidmarked skivvies. No use whatsoever, I bet."

He nodded in spite of himself.

"I'm not sure I understand. You said you didn't call earlier. Do you mean...," Keifer said.

"That's right," the woman added. "I decided on handling it myself." The policeman's ears perked. Oh, boy, he thought. Maybe we'd better go look. But the woman didn't seem anxious to walk back toward the enclosures anymore.

"Mrs. Dunwood. What happened tonight that you called the police," he asked quietly. Keifer carefully looked her in the eye. He did not want to corner her into aggravation.

The woman put her hand to her face coquettishly. Somehow, the movement worked. Now there was an iota of attractiveness about her. Keifer blinked, surprised by the result.

"Some come out here, you know, because it's me. Because they're afraid of me. Just want to mess with me, rile me up. That's what I've heard, anyhow."

"Heard from whom?" Keifer asked, uncertain what she was talking about. He was afraid of her, a little, himself.

"That idiot Willard down at The Joint. Sometimes I go out there. I'm no vegetarian. I sit at the bar and eat my burger and drink a Big Red. Willard talks to anyone, even me. The kids come in sometimes, want to see *the witch*. They call me that. Doesn't bother me so much. I mean, they're good church-going Baptists, so how bad can they be?" That one was aimed directly at Keifer and it stung a bit. He left it alone.

"But then they talk about me like I'm strange. Like I'm somehow at fault for what goes on around me. A pervert. So I don't go into town so much. I don't like being lied about, same as anyone else."

Keifer felt as if the muscles in his neck were useless and wriggly, from all of the nodding he was doing.

"I'll bet you didn't know that, did you," Mrs. Dunwood continued. "People coming here, just to look, just to taunt. Shouting hateful things, like you wouldn't imagine. I'll bet you didn't know. I'll bet if you did, you might have done something to stop it. I can sense that in you."

Strangely, as if she had never before done such a thing with anyone, she leaned forward tentatively and touched him on the bare arm below his uniform shirt sleeve. It was chilling and intimate at the same time and Keifer struggled not to flinch reflexively.

"Or maybe not," she snarled, the mood broken like an eggshell against a frying pan. This time Keifer did flinch. Her eyes seemed to glow. "Maybe you're like all of the others."

Keifer was stumped into silence again. A remote thought: what had happened to his quiet morning?

"Aaaaaaah!" came the cry. Behind Mrs. Dunwood, back in the cages and enclosures somewhere. Keifer's hand went to his flashlight.

"What? Was that?" he asked. He'd never heard an animal make a noise like that.

"Nothing," she said, trying to block his way.

"Excuse me, ma'am," he touched her shoulder to gently move around her. He felt something like a static shock in his fingertips. She didn't move. It was like pushing against a fencepost. He fell back on negotiation.

"Mrs. Dunwood. You need to let me see what's going on." Keifer said. "Now, please." He frowned at her.

"Animals aren't dumb, you know. They know how to

avoid things that are bad for them. Hunters and hunted. That's how the world is divided, but the hunted aren't *less* than those trying to hunt them, just because they might be weaker. Most know when they're being hurt. A bird that gets eaten by a cat knows it. But these were caged animals, trusting those cages, trusting me to protect them. And he'd been here more than once, you know. Thought he could come whenever he pleased, once he knew that the police weren't doing a damned thing."

Keifer resisted shaking his head in confusion. "He who, Mrs. Dunwood?" A chill wriggled down his backbone again. But then Mrs. Dunwood turned without responding. Her hair flowed out behind her above her nightgown. The ground mist covered her bare feet. She walked out of the manicured lawn, past cedar posts, into the animal enclosures.

He followed.

Tall fences of chicken cloth wired to one-inch galvanized pipe marked the left and right boundaries. He couldn't see what was in each cage and moved forward carefully. Again he noticed how clean it was and orderly. But it was a place of animals, and his nose was dulled by the constancy of the reek. She turned and stopped in front of one cage, different from the others. How? He glanced around. Ah, this one had wire across the top of the cage. Again Mrs. Dunwood read his thoughts.

"First time, I wasn't certain what had happened. My poor goat. Second time, it was one of her kids, not two months old. He ruined her. I had to put the poor damaged thing down myself."

Ruined her? Keifer thought. Ruined her how? Something went off in his head like a big *Oh.* Then his brain said *No way.* As if he wasn't a cop anymore, but was back being a kid going out to tip cows. Well, no wonder she's pissed. He stared into the dark enclosure, not at all sure what he was going to see – not sure what he was ready to see. Then something else came to him. This particular cage wasn't chicken-wire like the others, but chain-link. Steel hurricane fence - sides and top.

"Yeah, I switched out the fence, too," she said with cold satisfaction. "Damned fool didn't even notice."

"Oh, shit," Keifer finally grunted. This couldn't go well. The muscles in his pistol hand flexed instinctively, but he made them stay put. "In the cage."

"Yeah, and I snapped the lock behind him while he wasn't paying attention. Hunter and hunted. He'd come looking for her again, but I tricked him. You damn betcha I did." Her arms crossed triumphantly. Keifer's brow knitted - she'd caught some pervert. Well, now. Someone to arrest, he supposed. This was going to stink badly, he guessed. He stared at her. An odd thought flickered across the policeman's mind; that this was actually a handsome woman, someone of worth. Attractive even? No. Maybe. He tried to chase the idea away with one that said you're tired, it's been a long night and you're not thinking well, but in truth he could not.

Keifer slowly reached to his hip and pulled out his little flashlight again. With a thumb, he flicked on the beam. It was so bright, after trying to see in the darkness, in the moonlight, that his eyes stung, then ached as though he were driving into oncoming traffic. He pointed the flashlight into the enclosure. It was too tight a beam to take everything in and reflected back at him off of the chain-links.

In the cage was a man, lying on his side, naked. Again, Keifer suppressed the urge to pull his weapon. And the need to say something. There was blood around, a fair bit of it; bright on him and dark on the ground. It was difficult to tell how much of the blood was the man's own and what might have been someone or something else's blood. At least some of it was dribbling from the man's nose, which was bent to the side and looked broken. The man's eyes were swollen, but nothing was falling out of them, no dark and gruesomly gelatinous bits, thank goodness. Some of the blood also appeared to come from scrapes on the man's body, his side, knees, elbows and such. That the man was alive, but not well, Keifer could tell, but that was about all he could reasonably conclude by Triple A-Battery light. He scanned the rest of the enclosure. On the other side was an animal, bigger than he thought would be in there, also lying on its side.

"That's Billy," Mrs. Dunwood said. "He's just resting, I'll bet." Keifer scoped out the animal's mighty head with the eerie rectangularly slit-pupiled eyes and shaggy, mannish beard. The goat's horns wrapped and twisted around in a helix, encircling its ears in bony armor. Mrs. Dunwood leaned in close as if to see the same things that Keifer was. Her breath was sour but not unpleasant.

"Billy is one ornery bastard; I'll tell you that for nothing. He's the king-mean-boss of all goats. And he didn't like someone else doing his nanny-goats. So I put him in her enclosure, and when this fool came to visit, I just locked up behind him."

The woman leaned on the chain link fence, looking in the cage.

"The ancient Greeks found old billy goats to be such violent and randy animals they believed that they just had to have some human in them, and were probably possessed of some type of magic. They called them satyrs, and attributed

48

all sorts of misbehavior to them. Rape and deflowering and such. Well, not surprisingly, in addition to his nanny goats Billy here is partial to young billy goats, sheep, llamas, and just about anything that can't escape him when he's in such a mood. I suppose he had to bust this one around a bit before he could have his way, but eventually it all worked out. Turn-about is fair and all."

"Jesus," was all Keifer could say, nodding foolishly.

"Yeah, you'd think so," Mrs. Dunwood said. Keifer looked at her, questioningly. "Don't you see who it is?"

Keifer nodded one more time, but Mrs. Dunwood wasn't looking for his answer.

"The hypocritical old sycophant. Always casting the first stone and everything. Well, you want him, you got him."

Keifer held his breath. Did she mean the goat or the bloody mess lying on his side? He unsnapped his holster with a click, re-snapped it. He wasn't going to shoot any-thing, not yet, anyway. And he'd lied to Mrs. Dunwood. No, he couldn't tell who the naked, battered bastard was in the cage, not from here. And what was a sick-o-fant, anyway? He could only guess.

He tried to imagine all of the fuss. The out-of-town newspapers, once the story leaked, would make a field of hay of it. The talk back at the station. Just an inkling of what Mrs. Dunwood went through. He felt inclined to just leave him there, let things work themselves out, like she said.

Had he spoken out loud? Mrs. Dunwood replied as if he had.

"I can't help you there, officer. If I was in your shoes, I'd leave him there for a while at least. You don't want to mess around in Billy's cage, in case he aint quite had his fill. You want a cup of coffee?"

Keifer was not surprised to find that, suddenly, he did.

Night:

Woodrow the younger took his vorpal sword in hand;
that is, a glass of warm coke with a generous shot of Mescal
splashed on top, and climbed the carpeted stairs to the bedroom. Such a nice view from the expensive seats, he let the
voice in his head comment. Yes, it was still Woodrow senior's nasally baritone, of course, but if he didn't respond, it
couldn't go on, could it? He tip-toed past his sleeping,
arguably better half after looking at her carefully, her fore-arm
tangled in her soft locks as if pushing them from her face following a sweet pine tree whisperer breeze. She sleeps and
perchance dreams, he thought. Profound dreams that her
skin stays as smooth as the ridges of her brain, and for the
same lack-of-exposure reason. Dreams about Junior League
drama and the patient ripening of avocadoes. About being a
banker's wife, her life's perquisites made of silk and satin, not
off-the-rack, mind you. Oh, bunk, he whispers. She's in an
Ambien unconsciousness and isn't dreaming at all. He could
crank up a high-school band in the room and she'd barely
twitch. She sleeps to get away from all this. A bit player in a
tragedy, he thinks, as such things are measured: living
breathing humanity but with all of the intellectual foresight,
grasp or cognition of an invertebrate. A mollusk or perhaps
a jelly. That's about it.

If you can't tell the truth, even now, then to hell with
you, grumbled his father in his mind's ear. She is not the
problem, not substandard, not at fault. She is just *there*. She
was happy enough, once, before. You're the Atchison,
Topeka and Santa *fey* one here. For just once don't deflect,

don't judge, don't lie. Take one for the team. Woodrow felt his shoulders slump even more than usual. He couldn't even win an argument with himself. Sad, really, when you think about it.

He unbuckled his belt, undid the button to his trousers and unzipped them. Once upon a time, this activity, the very sound of this would inspire him to rigidity, because it was the standard, rather Pavlovian, auditory precursor to making love. Jingle-snick-zip. Oh what a relief it is! As reliable as... mesquite barbecue. Once, long ago, his wife would have been the focus of such sound vigor. Where oh where had those days gone? Silly question. He'd stopped paying attention to her. Stopped paying attention to much of anything. She'd been replaced by a series of discrete shapes and sizes. Was he a balloon with a microscopic pinprick, inexorably collapsing? Or was his manhood, part of the three-legged stool of his existence (including who he thought he was, and what other people thought of him,) meant to be long gone and well forgotten? He had a moment of relief, a spread of warmth throughout his chest. Everything about him had burst nearly simultaneously. Perhaps that was how it was for every man. He clearly deserved it. Did everyone?

Woodrow left on his gray boxers and white sleeveless undershirt, the so-called *wife-beater*, slipped his stocking'd feet into shower shoes, turned in the dark towards the half-full bed, tried to see his sleeping wife through the dark fur of night, failed. His once-queen, his judge and his jury for the moment, at least, and sometime guardian angel – so much responsibility - off duty.

He could only bear a moment of being in the same room with her so unencumbered, so he padded past the bed to the drapes, lifted them out of his way, took the handle of the sliding glass door and shoved mightily. With only a breath of noise, he was safely outside on the balcony. The night air had gone still now and just cool enough for a tickly rise of goose-flesh on his arms. He sipped his cocktail and held it in his mouth, the bite and cloy of it dancing on the parquet floor of his tongue. The night-eyes of a car flickered through the tall gray peonies at the Belgian-block curb of the yard, approached, arrived and safely passed. Woodrow smirked. The town's fairy godfathers had not anticipated that the rabble would wrap around the elite and the reward of such a planning gap was that workaday-Dads made the Subaru run to Target to fetch fresh disposable *didies* for their spawn right through his no longer upper, just crusty neighborhood. Or else, the blue-vested hefalumps coming home from the late shift offering of *fryzwithat* chugged back the other way. There was no such thing as truly quiet anymore.

He leaned against the black cast-iron railing, grasping the metal with his free hand. It was neither cool nor warm. The day's sun was absorbed by it, and now it had released much of that energy back in predictable Newtonian thermodynamic law.

He wondered if all men lived in a tragic-hero saga of their own design and manufacture. The Bail-Wolf, howling at the door, waiting to serve. The queen of clumps, snoring soundly inside, unaware. And he, with no heroic function whatsoever.

He cocked his arm - without draining the cocktail, those of you still keeping score - and flung his aptly named tumbler as far as he was able, out into the void-that-wasn't-really-a-void, and then waited. Waited for that oh-so satisfying splash of broken glass to bounce off of his eardrums. Waited...

Dark:

Patterson stepped off of the gritty concrete sidewalk and into the grass. He stood and wiggled his toes, scrunching the unfettered coolness, savoring it. The feeling swept him back. Teenaged. No, even before that. Young enough to just enjoy being barefoot on a Saturday morning, sniffing the salad-green perfume of just-mown grass.

His mom's front lawn had been small, bigger than a postage stamp but still too small even for a two-to-a-side pick-up game of football. Contrary to normal-child behavior, he'd liked helping her around some. Mom had been a book-keeper – as a journalist he loved that word with its three con-secutive double-taps on the typewriter – back when not many women were. Possibly from pushing that Sisyphean rock, she often came home from her day of work worn out and cranky. So he completed his homework without being asked. Policed up his room and made his bed. He could have made his own supper fish-sticks, too, but she forbade him to use the oven when she wasn't home. She kept the reel mower hanging in the back shed attached to the house, so he had learned how to wheedle it off the wall hook and could work it if he leaned against the handle with all of his strength, to get the blades spinning. But his old Chuck Taylor knock-offs were more plastic than rubber-bottomed and they slid on the grass, so he kicked them off when he mowed the lawn. His toes dug into the turf – if crabgrass and dandelions could be called some-thing so *country club* as turf – and he fretted and sweated the machine back and forth, watching the hoppers try to stay ahead of the spinning mechanical shears. What on blue-eyed earth are you thinking? she shouted at him when she first saw him green-footed, sitting on the front step. You might cut off your toes! But she was pleased, he knew, in her grumpy fashion.

On the dark grass, neatly edged, he wiggled his digits. He pushed away the sudden thought that this was where the imbeciles in the neighborhood walked their dogs, crapping and peeing to their canine hearts' content. Or worse, that this was the place where simpering, put-upon spouses walked their pets with plastic bags to fetch the doo home afterwards. The thought wouldn't push: wasn't getting up to go into the office enough? Taking complaint calls from customers enough, writing copy, writing content, writing strained, choked sentences, sitting in conference rooms staring at charts and analyzing metrics and absorbing the drone of motivational buzz-words, enough? Didn't that daily level of mind-numbing, teeth-grinding *mundanity* un-man one sufficiently? Or was feces-fetching just the *grand-mal* icing on the cake? A habit you developed before experimenting with various types of post-midlife crisis fixes. Like seeking out a nineteen-year-old with a daddy complex. Or tasting the barrel of a pistol held in your mouth.

Behave! Patterson's mind scolded itself. Just finish your strange little walk. A cooler than expected breeze wafted past his ancient-boxered junk, simultaneously tickling and shriveling him. If Madolyn chose to wake right then – an exercise in the suspension of disbelief already – and reached for him on the bed next to her, and finding that space empty sat up and looked around, and not seeing him got out of bed and didn't find him in the house, but remembered that she had kicked his dirty laundry left on the bedroom floor and so looked out the front door to find him schlepping the neighborhood in his undies and wife-beater, she would be particularly and peculiarly unhappy with him.

That was for certain.

Big Dogs (Barking)

The thin whistle and sudden ground-burst next to him sent Patterson spilling forward. Shards of glass whickered in the night air. His palms skidded on the concrete and just missed catching him from bashing his face on the ground with a thud. *Damn! What the...?* He tried to clamber back to his feet, but his head hurt and didn't and then did again, and he'd lost his boxers in the urgency of his emergency dive, and now, strapped about his thighs, they prevented a prudent, graceful recovery. His...sensitives...were pressed unpleasantly against the abrasive sidewalk and he didn't feel much like popping thoughtlessly to his feet, trying to pretend that nothing happened. *Double-damn!* This was a bit of conundrum. On the other hand, there was just as much of a chance that there was further artillery in the offing, launched heedlessly into the night, might at this moment be following the same trajectory as the first.

Get up, he told himself. Now.

Dessert: Churros and coffee:

Apparently, the restaurant wishes to close. They don't say anything but the message is not terribly subtle. Smith sits up from his food-induced torpor like one of those frogs that buries itself in the mud during the dry season, then climbs out following a downpour unaware of how many months or even years have passed. He – Smith not the frog – notices the music is now off, chairs are stacked upside-down atop tables. Instead of appetizingly fried meat, there is the hint of an acrid tinge of pine cleanser in the air. He checks his watch. Ten after ten. Time for them to get going. Shouldn't play around like this, taking this long to get a meal. Keifer must be pissed.

Has he fallen asleep (again Smith, not Keifer), his belly

full of chow? How long, oh Lord, how long? drones the refrain of the book of lamentations in Smith' mind's ear. Why is each shift an interminably extended, yet chiefly eventless chain of uncountable minutes?

His gears engage. Get up, he tells himself. Go talk to the girl. He looks at her, sitting at the cash register, looking back at him. Lovely. Get up and go talk to her. She is right over there. Easy. Talk to her. He looks back at his plate after she tucks a loose lock of her hair behind her ear. She's smart, and kind, and has a real life, not just the one you invade when you're hungry. Ask her about it. What do you have to lose?

No. If she wanted him to talk to her, she...would do something that gave him a clearer message. For all his deductive reasoning, he doesn't know what that clue might entail. Back in school, he wasn't popular, wasn't one of the cool kids. Nothing since has improved on that record. He is empirically certain that women don't want men to come up and just start talking to them. To those men who do, however, whose tone-deafness or foolhardiness overrides good sense, they will be polite. They will smile and talk back and recite pleasantries and all the time they will be thinking leave me alone leave me alone leave me alone.

Creep.

And so, for Smith, inexorable, ineffable, unseeable time drags on and presses down on him, leans on his shoulders with a gravity as palpable and opposite end of the mood spectrum as the pleasant weight of the chimichanga in his gut. Nothing seems likely to pull him out of the tailspin of sameness, one evening after another. Is this karmic punishment for some offense in a previous life? What to do, then? Is there some other payment he can make to right the scale?

Not that he actually believes such off-kilter thought-systems –
but he occasionally reaches out, figuratively, to try and snare
such pre-camel-back-breaking straws. Just in case.

He hauls himself back from that empty, improbable spot
in the future that resides about twelve inches from his head
upon which he has been concentrating his otherwise mind-
less stare to glance over at Ludlow. His partner is busy nosh-
ing on the second of three cinnamon *churros* on the
communal plate Serena brought to them after their meals.
Their hostess? Sitting at the front of the place, reading.
Nope – not reading anymore. Just sitting in the quiet.
Lovely. And no one seems to be troubled that they are still
there. OK, good. Nothing is happening anywhere else. He
stares at the dessert-plate.

When viewed end-on, churros look like stars. As if someone used an old child's toy to form them, to press them out
of a mold and snip them off with blunt plastic scissors. Each
bite is a sweet and spicy star-bite of fried dough. Nibbling
away at the cosmos. Ludlow mows through them without
thinking, as if they were the only thing between him and the
utterly endless flavor void. Staving off starvation. The last
tasty tidbits he'll ever consume on Earth. He always eats two
of three, then asks Smith if he wants his. Ludlow's fingertips
are presently coated with sugar and cinnamon as well, so of
course they need to be licked, one deliberately after another.
Only then does he wipe his hands on a napkin. He sighs at
the ecstasy of the final delicacy, and then looks over at the
big man, simultaneously catching Smith in his reverie, and
feeling sheepish at being watched while he eats. But no,
Smith is not looking at him, but doing his zone-out thing.
He's somewhere else, completely. And then, suddenly, he is
here, so Ludlow launches into his cockamamie sales pitch.

"What?" Ridiculously innocent. Slightly defensive.

"Nothing," says Smith, true to form and on-brand.

"You want your dessert?"

"No."

"You sure?"

"Yeah, I'm sure."

"They're very good, you know."

"I do know," says Smith. "We've been here before."

"You should try it." Ludlow ignores the snarkiness. "Just once in your life."

"No. Thanks."

"May I?" He points at the final treat.

"I don't care."

"You sure?"

"I swear, Ludlow. I've never been more certain of anything."

"Alright." Ludlow fights back, as he always does, the urge to sulk. Smith can hear it in his voice, even with only these brief word-clues. The young man is just trying to be friendly, to find a way in, to discover something they possess other being two different people spending a lot of time together. And although they do have that in common and little else, it wouldn't be a sin to just...what? Be partners? Protect and serve? Have each other's back?

How hard is it to *just be there*?

The big man slumps. Shit, goes his interior monologue. Just eat the damned donut. Ludlow is right. It won't kill you. As if it is someone else's, he watches his hand reach out and take the thing between thumb and forefinger, just before Ludlow grabs it himself. He doesn't respond to Ludlow's surprised smile at this...playfulness. Smith lifts the churro to his mouth and takes a tentative bite. The star-points of toasted flour and egg and salt and water and granular sugar scuff the roof of his mouth. But the infusion of butter and cinnamon make his mouth water so it might actually leak from the corners of his lips. He chews noisily.

"Mmm."

"Good, right?" Ludlow triumphantly slaps the table top with the flat of his hand.

"Mmm." The world's most noncommittal approval noise.

"Ahem..."

Smith' head snaps around. Serena is standing there, next to him. She smiles, slightly. How did she arrive here so...unnoticed? Were his eyes closed while he chewed? She smells like lavender infused shampoo and...electricity. No, that last is something he imagines.

"Would you like more?" Serena asks, her voice low and gentle. As if she is talking to a child. He takes no offense at the thought. "The kitchen always makes an extra batch to take home. So it won't go to waste. The dough, you know?"

Smith cannot speak. His mouth is suddenly glued shut, dry and sticky-sweet.

"I'll get a couple" she says, rescuing him from his silence. "Put 'em in a bag for later. You do get hungry later, right?"

Smith can only nod. If he opens his mouth, cinnamon-sugar will spill out onto his uniform shirt. Speak and he will spray happy-food debris at her.

Serena turns and walks away. If Smith could punch himself in the face for being a nitwit, he would do it.

Ludlow leans back on his creaky chair, crosses his arms, smiles, but nips the side of his tongue between his molars to remain silent. Don't spoil it, he tells himself. Let it be.

Serena returns and sets the bag on the table, along with

their check. She smiles again, this one for Smith only.

"Whenever you're ready. No rush." She goes to put away her textbook.

Ludlow stifles a grin for the man who isn't his friend, isn't his partner, but is still *something*.

Smith shakes his head, but his eyes crinkle at the corners. Yeah, I know, they say. OK, then. You win, skinny man.

Dispatch crackles on the tactical radio attached to Smith's shoulder epaulet. It is such a surprise, he turns his head and answers with his mouth full, dribbling sugar onto the microphone.

Gloomy, with a chance of incoming cocktail glasses:

Younger Woodrow (as far as he knew, lesser in every way such things can be gauged), returned quietly to the kitchen, fetched another dram of liquid courage, toddled back past his unconscious wife to the bedroom balcony, tipped it back and drained it, swallowed with lip-smacking satisfaction, and launched the glass out into the never-never. That first crash had been mostly gratifying – a semi-distant pop and tinkle – if not exactly what he'd expected. He'd requested of the gods a hand-grenadesque explosion. He wished that he had shouted "Fuck you, dear Father," when he flung it, but for reasons he couldn't explain – for Woodrow certainly considered those particular words in that particular order often enough – he had not. The tequila he'd poured into his belly was burning its way outward to his extremities, like a glorious alcohol-infection. The second throw of fine etched-leaded crystal smashed to whatever the glass equivalent of flinders were. He pounded the iron rail of the balcony with his fist and gave a muted *whoop*. Fun! This was fun. Or maybe this wasn't actually fun, except when compared with everything else his life had been for so many months that if it were a pregnancy it would result in the breach birth of a white whale of misery. Woodrow didn't care, not at the moment, not right now. Fun enough. Let's do it again. He turned to fetch another drink-bomb, but something wended its audible way up from the darkness of the street below, filtering through the semi-drunken haze.

"Asshole!"

Patterson had shimmied off of the sidewalk, to his knees, poked little bits of sharp pebbles or possibly glass into them, and still couldn't quite balance himself and pull up his boxers. His privates withered in the night air. Thank whatever gods found this entertaining that no one walked by, tugging along their corgies or pugs or toxic-waste, land-mine-creating golden retrievers.

Jesus love the little children, he just couldn't get himself off the ground.

The newspaperman suddenly remembered something, a moment a million moments ago. Standing on the sidelines before half-time. He'd been no player – such an achievement might have made all the difference in the world, or meant nothing at all – but was a cornet in the band. Now wait a minute; a cornet wasn't too bad. It was some number of steps above clarinet. It wasn't *tuba*. But, then, of course it was. For although within band there was instrumental nuance containing many sub-levels of society – concert and marching, first and second and beyond chairs, precious solo assignments – outside band, in the real world, it was all the pale nerdy sometimes out of tune singularity called band. Chubby cheeked girls with stringy hair and skinny chicken-head-eating geek boys, each and every one.

Anyhow, way back on that, dare he call it fateful, Friday night, there had been an event. A big manchild catching the opposing team's punt. Working up a head of steam, chugging up the field, heading for the sidelines, where the marching band was awaiting halftime, all prepared to do a complicated *South Pacific* medley with the brass section as ocean waves crashing on the sandy shore. Here he came, ball tucked safely in the crook of his arm, as big as life, and the defenders gathered to pin him down, to wall him up like the cask of Amontillado, be the rocky shoreline for him to break on. Patterson could still recall how fierce he was in his white helmet, his grass-stained jersey and pants, his cleated feet like the hooves of a great stallion. What he wouldn't have given up to have been that young man, that creature watched by everyone in the stands, all willing him towards the end zone.

As the play approached the sidelines, with all the pent up and released energy, the rumble and crash and fractal chaos of it, the band shrank back into itself. The big fellow carrying the ball galloped ahead of his teammates, churning up turf and chewing up yards. The opposing team gathered before him, herding, steering him to the edge of the field. Right here! Patterson-in-that-moment thought. In front of them! He shrank back even more, and bumped into Shelley McWhorter standing behind him. Shelley was one of the baton twirlers – not one of the two lead baton twirlers, currently in the news again over some never lain to rest issue from oh so many years gone by, but one of the rank-and-file twirlers whose assets were nevertheless rather prominent - and when he bumped into her she made a noise like a cat does when its tail gets trod upon. Ms McWhorter's screech of indignance carried above and through all the other noise to him and he whirled around approximately one hundred

eighty degrees to see what had happened to cause such a
sound similar to the legato 17-note rising diatonic scale for
clarinet at the start of Gershwin's Rhapsody in Blue - had
he caused someone to break a reed? – and perhaps also to
preemptively apologize (something band members often did,
because it saved time) but before he could she hauled off and
bopped him on the shako with the rubber tip of her baton.
It didn't hurt him, but it did dent his uniform hat. That in
itself wasn't important, wasn't the crux of this anecdote, but
caused Patterson to flinch backwards again (even though he
could remember to this very day the wondrous soft, warm
and receptive feeling of Shelley McWhorter's rather de-luxe
bosom even through her sequins-spangled uniform and his
own unspangled wool band-suit. Nearby, barely audible over
the thunderous noise of the crowd, the rumble of approach-
ing cleats, and the shouting of the coaches and players, a
youngster was holding a Swinger transistor radio by its wrist
leash and that radio was broadcasting a song. The Doors'
Jim Morrison warbling "Hello, I love you! Won't you tell me
your name?" and the uncanny logic of its relevance and
timing scribed those words and that tune on the hard granite
wall of his memory so that he always associated it with this
moment. He experienced an auditory-tactile *affection* event
of historic amplitude - yet another term of endearment,
enthrallment and measurement that could be applied to
Shelley's tits - something young idiot-children of today would
never experience - not with unlimited access to all of the
flickering online porn in the electronic universe.) In retreating away from the possibility of Shelley clocking him once
again, perhaps more successfully, with her baton, the now
facing backwards-to-the-oncoming conflict Patterson had also
jostled his bandmates - the third and fourth-chair trumpets –

and they stumbled onto the field. Mind, it was only the edge of the field, barely over the chalk sidelines, but it was not yet halftime, and the punt return play being attempted by the big man in the white helmet and prevented by the many large members of the opposition were converging on this same unfortunate parcel of real-estate.

The fourth (and even-a-half)-chair trumpet, sporting a cold sore which significantly affected his embouchure (and, rather more completely, the hopes of his high-school social life) saw things as they unfolded, and let go of his trumpet (a Conn with sticky pistons and a dented bell his parents rented by the month theoretically that there would be only thirty days wasted if he ever stopped making that noise in his room only somewhat vaguely recognizable as Leroy Anderson's *Sleigh Ride*) and tucked into a ball like a cartoon armadillo, intending to be safely kicked away from any danger. The third-chair fell over his bandmate and released his own Etude instrument at apogee, so that it flipped end-over-end in the direction of the young man in the white helmet with the ball. The football player jinked to dodge the golden projectile coming into his field of vision (rather limited by the cross-bars of his helmet,) while anticipating the actions of the on-coming crowd of angry defenders. That was the extent of his cerebral bandwidth for planning ahead – all other compo-nents of his brain activity fully engaged with the tasks of breathing, blinking, running, holding onto the ball, and those auto-magic functions of keeping his heart beating and bladder and bowels from releasing. It had no remaining ca-pacity for discerning what the rolled-up thing in the band uniform in his way at sideline's edge was doing, nor what he should do about it. Then that other band-uniform thing top-pling over the rolled-up band-uniform thing took the last bit of empty turf. OK, then. Time to stop. In the big man-boy's defense, he tried to but couldn't. So, with almost no ergs of thought energy allocated to the task, he considered changing direction, made a quick panoramic glance, but each and all of those alternatives were worse, filled with more band-uniform things and some cheerleadery sweater-and-skirt things. In an instant, muscle memory informed him that space and time had run out and he would now have to run over them, run them over, whichever was the correct grammar for such an event. His knees kept pumping, his arms wrapped around the ball, still cradling it protectively (don't don't don't fumble!) as he entered the traffic of sideline. His huge, heavy left foot planted on the hand of the fourth-plus-chair trumpet, who made a noise similar to Shelley McWhorter's bleat, although his was far louder due to fact that the extreme pain of having a cleated shoe snap the bones of three different important brass instrument-playing fingers is probably worse than a boob-poking. It was not a firm footing, either, and that was a shame on many levels, because now the big young man in the white helmet found his balance compromised. He stuck out his other foot to stem the fall and at that moment his knee was hit by the falling Etude trumpet, which sent it spinning back towards the sidelines and he collided with the avalanche of players on the opposing team, buried as surely as a skier in an mountainside snowdrift. He howled as he disappeared, because his ankle – the one attached to the foot which had stepped on the band nerd's hand, was twisting beneath him in a way not intended by nature when it created via evolution the hinge joint which permitted two types of movement only in one plane – *plantarflexion* and *dorsiflexion.*

The crowd was so loud now that the Doors tune couldn't

be heard anymore and then-Patterson didn't know why, because he was still facing the young woman with her decorative weapon of mass half-time entertainment. Shelley McWhorter was looking past him, though, so he peeked over his shoulder to see a spinning hunk of brass coming his way. Somehow, with a lithe athleticism that eluded him forever after, he ducked. The trumpet floated toward on its way past, end over end, its momentum, or was it inertia? increased by the energy provided it during the collision with the young ballcarrier's knee. A fleeting thought...the trumpet, if it missed him, would hit the just shy of lovely Shelley McWhorter. Maybe in the face. Maybe in the chest!

No.

Patterson stuck his hand up as the projectile went past. He had no track record of success in such chivalric endeavors. Sugar bowls tumbled out of cabinets at home, apples from open lunchboxes, pencils always skittered beneath distant radiators. But this time, just this once in a long undistinguished line of failure, his thumb, that opposable arbiter of sapient development, painfully caught the brunt of the trumpet's flying brass bell and deflected it away from the baton-twirler. She saw it go, too. She then looked down at him, and for a transitory moment she smiled, knowing what he just did to protect her from bodily harm. Of course, she then also rather uncharacteristically assembled the entirety of the moment's chaos into a cause-and-effect event, and pinned all guilt on him, mostly negating any heroism on his part on her part. But still....

Patterson rolled uncomfortably onto his hip and pushed himself up, hauling up his boxer shorts as he stood. Well, alright then. If he had had a helmet on, he would have tipped it jauntily over one brow. If he weren't standing there, barefoot in his underwear, on the sidewalk far down the street from his own house, blood and sweat dripping from his brow, he might have felt that sense of satisfaction, that he was someone who could actually do things, right and good, for more than just a handful of questionably steady heartbeats. It was, however, enough time to *take a stand.*

"Hey, you asshole!" he shouted into the absorbent dark. "You could have hurt someone!"

Woodrow might have been able to stop from launching a third empty cocktail tumbler, if he hadn't just consumed its contents and lost just that last bit of strength, dexterity, and the so-called flinch mechanism necessary for quick reaction. He heard the shout from below, was adequately surprised by it, assimilated the message, and was insufficiently responsive to its unspoken imperative.

"Oh, yeah?" he replied with enough volume to waft over the neighborhood. "Fuck you!" He leaned back, with hands on hips and nodded. It was most satisfying.

Patterson recoiled but didn't flop as the next cocktail tumbler once again ex-and-imploded on the street nearby. Instead, he stepped into the street and crouched, using the ten inches of curb as meager protection. The *plash* of expensive glass wasn't so close as before, so that was good. He looked up and saw the shimmer of crystal in the nearest streetlight. Not thrown at him, but near enough to give pause. Perhaps not trying to hit him at all. Still, if this was going to be more than a war of words, he was going to need both ammunition and a target, or he was going to need to beat a hasty retreat. Which he didn't want to do but saw no other choice.

Eyes clenched nearly shut, he reached out his fingers, grasping for something to throw. A grit-covered stone, the right size and weight for heaving. Perfect. No. He gave it a tentative sniff. Petrified, calcified, sun-dried dog-doo, ancient and dusty. He went to fling it away, thought twice. Hauled back and heaved it towards the house. Ha! Found another coprolith. Flung.

"Take that, you bastard!" he shouted, suddenly hoping it wasn't actually God, because throwing shit at the *Almighty* couldn't go well. He searched for more.

Disturbance call - responding:

Smith and Ludlow walk one notch quicker than swiftly to their prowler. The big man unlocks the doors and they slide in. Ludlow reflects again for just a moment about how he wishes again they still had the 380, for moments just like this, but he bites off his frustration and doesn't let the thought leak out of his head as words. No one gives points for getting such things right, but there you are. What did his granddad say? *If wishes were horses, beggars might ride.* He thinks he knows what that means. You can't have what you can't have. Isn't that applicable, right now? It sure seems right. He reaches back and tucks his wallet deeper into his trousers pocket, in that way one might if he were walking through a sketchy neighborhood. Then he checks the snap on his holster. Secure.

Smith acknowledges the call from Clara in Dispatch and finds he is still savoring the remaining particles of spicy sweet of the surprisingly fine churro. Selena's gift bag of a couple more sits beside him on the seat. He and Ludlow can share these later – perhaps just before shift end. He switches on the blue-white light bar and backs out of the restaurant parking lot. Only when they are heading down the street does he turn on the siren. Silly thing, this particular rule. Always engage the siren when on a possible criminal call. So you can never sneak up on a burglar. It is counterintuitive. Not to mention, there is no traffic on the street to get out of their way, and it's damned late – the siren is way too noisy. Some-one's bound to complain. But it's the rule, and he and Lud-low follow the rules.

Now.

He knows that Ludlow wants to barrel through town – breaks in their patrol boredom are few and far between. Still, Smith maintains a prudent speed, slows at the traffic lights not yet on overnight blinking yellow and red. Domestic disturbance, called in by a neighbor. These can be the easiest situations to handle, or the worst. Husbands and wives in disagreement with one another, their fight ostensibly private, suddenly redirecting all of their anger and frustration towards the new problem of public law enforcement at their door. Those involved are suddenly embarrassed that anyone heard what they were going through and thought it required some additional and uninvited audience. Or they are drunk – never in a good and fun way, if there is such a thing – and can't communicate clearly what the problem is. Cannot help but exacerbate the situation. All of which sounds like a comedy and almost never is.

Ludlow toggles the radio and calls dispatch to confirm that they are *en route* and to double-check the address. He frowns and repeats it back. Correct. Looks over at Smith, who predictably, doesn't shrug. He clicks off the siren and lights as they enter the grid-and-curve of residential streets and avenues that make up the wealthier section of Garrison. If there's really nothing wrong, no one will mind that every grand muckity-muck in town doesn't know about this call. And if there is something awry, well, pretty much the same

Tall shade oaks blended with groomed hedges – you can

tell the lawns are immaculate even in the gloom of night. Widely spaced streetlamps drop perfect yellow cones of light. He and Ludlow both hum their windows down, sniffing the sweet pine-needle humidity of the East Texas night, and listen for trouble. It is noisy with the whine of insects, peaceful. They roll down the street, eyes peeled.

The rock *slams* against the hood of the prowler, chipping off black paint and leaving a pinky-tip sized divot. Ludlow, in an effort to duck, slides off of the seat to the passenger-side floor and can see nothing. *Holy crap* Smith accidentally hits the gas and brakes simultaneously and with equal foot-poundage and the enormous prowler engine screams as do the tires as the vehicle bounds and swivels sideways across the street before hopping the curb. He has that "oh, no, not again" sensation ripple across the front curtain of his consciousness and intentionally chooses to take his foot off the gas and stop trying to proceed. The engine conks out. Oh, well, good enough. Better to stay here, for now. His eyes flicker across the dark tableau, see nothing untoward.

What the hell. He cracks the door and the interior lamp comes on. Sees a faint glitter on the hood. So not a rock. Glass, maybe? Heavy. Thrown. Is this the domestic disturbance call, or something else entirely?

Ludlow is trying to climb up off the passenger side floor and unsnap his holster. He is frightened and embarrassed that he is frightened and frightened that he is embarrassed. This jumble of emotions prevents him finding the necessary dexterity key to unsnapping his holster and bringing his weapon to bear on the situation.

Smith gives him a hand up from his predicament onto the bench seat by the scruff of his neck and hisses at Ludlow to keep his gun in place. "Slow," he says. He swings open the driver door and stays low behind it, hunkered down on his haunches. Lyrics from an old song earworm on him like a scratched 45 - *just remember there's a lot of bad and beware!* His shoes rustle the grass beneath. Jesus, we're up on someone's lawn. That's going to be a pain in the ass later. Why can't anything go easy?

The 1963 T-Bird chase:

The newspaperman sat on the cool Belgian-block granite of the curb and felt his big toe. It was a bulbous appendage at the end of all-things-Patterson that rarely received any attention at all from him, so it was difficult to determine the cause of its toe-woes, but he assumed he had inadvertently stepped on a shard of the projectile leaded crystal. Bad luck if you measure such things, as the person tossing the glasses certainly wasn't actually trying to hit him, and hadn't thrown too many, unless this sort of thing was going on every night and this was cumulative glass, scattered like landmines in the Korean peninsula DMZ. Of course, this observation seemed highly unlikely. Still, there you were: your butt cool and your toe hot. He pressed on the end of it, down where he needed his toenail clipped and felt the sting, and his fingertips were sticky with oozing, high-alcohol content blood. Pain! Blood!

"My God!" he squealed, too loudly.

"There is no God," came a voice from above. Ha! He knew it. This was a test!

"I'm bleeding!" he replied, his voice catching in his throat a little bit.

"Be thankful of the blood of life. It is proof you're still alive."

Well, Patterson thought. Only God would know this and that was good enough for him. He began to weep with joy and also the throb in his toe. So he'd finally found God's house. He'd always suspected it was around here, some-where. He pulled up the sweaty tail of his undershirt to blot his eyes. At that moment a monster roared and screamed to-wards him from the dark of the street. The Devil himself, here to continue the examination, arriving all brimstone and burning flame. He closed his eyes, held his barking dogs, and prayed.

Woodrow winged his sixth dead soldier out into the night air. In a moment of process efficiency management, he'd put them on a tray - one of his wife's brass chargers - along with the liquor, so he didn't have to make so many trips. Each missile had been a drink first, before launching. Now he wiped his brow. All done. Just in time, too. His arm was getting tired, he'd heaved the last of his wife's crystal and had no interest in going back to the kitchen to look for the everyday drinking accoutrements. So he took the half-full bottle of booze by the neck and gave it a wing as well. Then he joyfully frisbee'd the brass charger. Woodrow felt the wobble in his legs that foretold the early onset of global swarming and yet he was remarkably content. From below he divined the shouting, screeching hubbub, questioning the divine and the mortal, but attributed all that to more voices in his head. After all, he deserved voices in his head, same as anyone else. Surely, he had achieved some critical level of stress that created such phenomena. A sudden consideration burst into the foreground of his mind. A drive was all he needed, to clear his head, maybe even feel like a grown man again. To give him *perspective*. He abruptly about-faced and swung open the balcony door to commence the arduous task of finding his car keys.

Big Dogs (Barking)

Smith sees the man hunkered down in the dark gutter and assesses the situation. Is this the man who threw the glass? What the hell. He looks like he might be drunk. Is he wearing any clothing? Boxer shorts, and a tee-shirt pulled up to his face. Like a mask? He appears to be barefoot, reaching down and playing with his feet. Somewhere out of the light there is the crash-tinkle of a bottle – a familiar sound. Is someone shooting at bottles? No gunshot noise. Then something new: a cymbal clash, like that sound a drummer makes after a bad joke. A rim-shot. This place has gone *spooky*, he thinks. Still, Smith doesn't pull his weapon. Instead he turns the prowler's single-spot in that direction. It may be a bad idea – a spotlight is a target for a shooter. If this doesn't work out, he'll be in a world of trouble for breaking that rule. He motions Ludlow to remain down and in place, hopes for the best in that regard, and then stands. The underclad man raises his head, eyes closed, mumbling quietly. Is he praying? Carefully, Smith scans him with the beam of his spot, sees the blood on his face and hands. Oh boy. Ludlow turns back on the prowler's light-bar, which strobes blue and white, opens the passenger door and crouches behind it, peering through the window with the radio transmitter mic in his hand. Smith shakes his head. Well, terrific. Here we are, big as life.

"Sir, this is the police. Are you alright?"

Patterson grimaced. Not the devil at all. Just the local constabulary. He sniffed, took in his own humid, coppery, dog-flop reek. No devil means no god, either, flinging crystalline, omniscient attention down on him. He took a breath and heard the wheeze, but his chest felt surprisingly un-heart-attacky. So why does my head hurt, unless I am dying and this is the white light I should go towards? He'd bitten his tongue, badly. He expectorated bloody spit down the front of his shirt. He lurched to his feet, which now hurt like the dickens, but in a distant sort of way. Distant dickens. *Hee!* Speaking of which, his own particular privates had an ache to them as well. He wondered why, but couldn't discern a reason. This is not my night at all, he decided.

"Sir, hold it right there. Stay where you are, please." Smith firmly instructs as he steps out from behind the door of the prowler. Blood on his face, blood on his shirt, the fellow is walking barefoot in broken glass. And he holds out his empty hands, imploring with bloody fingertips. "Stay where you are," Smith repeats, a notch louder, holding out his own empty hands. No gun, he told himself. Not this time.

"Jeez," Ludlow hisses from his seat. He wants to say a lot more, but is doing his best to hold it in. This whole mess is a great deal like a horror movie, especially seen in the strange blue flicker that the light-bar provides. Blood and moaning and half-dressed weirdos with unexplained behaviors. The word pops unbidden into Ludlow's head – *zombie* · and unconsciously he touches the safety snap of his holster with his free hand. Then he hears the distant rumble of thunder. No, not thunder. Something else. He sees Smith turn towards the house and follows his gaze.

In flip-flopped feet, Woodrow flattened the gas pedal to the floor, revving the engine on the '63 Thunderbird. The ancient Detroit Big Muscle Iron speed-beast rattled the walls of the garage, kicking up its heels, spewing a plume of exhaust into the enclosed space, that marvelous old-school stench of leaded gasoline. He let off the gas and felt the

growl up from his arch to his ankle and along his hamstring
to his knee. It didn't purr but rumbled like an angry thing
preparing to jump. *I missed this*, he whispered beneath the
noise. The cloth that had covered the old beauty was on the
floor. Dust mixed with the fumes. He coughed. I missed
this, he repeated in a croak.

He groaned the gear into reverse. Slowly released the
clutch. Gave the beast some gas and felt her buck beneath
him like a bronco. The Thunderbird's back bumper hit the
garage door – closed – at about two miles per hour, but the
undeniable science of mass and potential energy becoming
kinetic took precedence over the inertia of the painted three-
eighth's inch plywood, splintering and thusly removing it as
an obstacle with only minor crumpling of the bumper's
chrome. It was a loud event, however, a mix of engine roar
and breaking wood. Woodrow smiled as he flopped back
and forward in the driver's seat.

Smith hears the crash, and because he is already nervous
and jerky about smashing glass and strange, unresponsive,
bloody men and the whining insect nighttime and simply not
getting this wrong and being called on the carpet and having
to hear about it all one more time, or worse, one *last* time, he
bellies out on the lawn. Unfortunately, in taking this action
the holster of his firearm is beneath him, pinned against his
hip. Damned thing.

Ludlow, stealing another look out from behind the passenger door, sees his partner suddenly go down, out of sight,
and is horrified. Tears spring to his eyes for all of the crappy
things he has thought about Smith just this evening – that he
is annoying and bossy and really not so much better than he
although Smith maintains a constant air of superiority over

him. Of course Smith is better; a better policeman and, dare he say it? a better friend. Damn! Tonight he even tasted a churro!

That's it.

Ludlow wipes his eyes with the sleeve of his uniform, holds the radio microphone to his mouth and keys dispatch.

"Officer down," he hisses, but to his dismay he has pulled the cord out of the mic. "Shit," he says and finds the snap on his holster, pulls the piece and slips out from behind the door. What is that screaming noise? Where is that zombie?

Stars spun in Woodrow's head as it bashed the steering wheel and swung back again.

"Damn, tha' hur..." he gurgled as the T-bird danced down the driveway and into the street with the crushed garage door folded over its tail like a Carnivale mask. By some happenstance, Woodrow swung the wheel, accidentally depressing the horn-bar with a mighty bark, and the iron stallion responded by taking the turn with a squeal of tires and was now heading with some speed towards the others.

Backwards.

Patterson tried to turn to see what this new noise was but his legs were twisted so that he was leaning too far forward, reaching with a mostly silent beseeching of the policeman to please catch him. But the policeman dove to the ground. *Ah, too bad,* he thought as he fell on top of the man.

Smith' face bashes into the turf. Ouch. The crazy fellow in boxers and tee-shirt falls atop him like an old tree in the forest. Smith gasps and takes in a snootful of sand, dust and old lawn clippings. Something else, too. Dog crap. He coughs spasmodically, a two-dollar word Patterson would appreciate if he weren't lying on top of him. And ironically enough, Smith would reciprocally appreciate not actually having Patterson on top of him, so that he can breathe and/or cough sufficiently to get dirt and other stuff out of his bronchia and air in. It is a difficult, complex moment.

Ludlow, .357 Magnum Colt Python drawn and two-hand Weaver-stanced in the direction of the ragged-red-lighted, garage-wreckage covered, and reverse-geared Thunderbird, gives the moment its proper due. He should first inform the driver that he is going to shoot if he doesn't stop the automobile instantly. Yet, he knows that such a warning is a fool's errand, as no one could possibly hear anything he has to say over the engine roar, the sparky-scraping of scrap-garage-door metal on the pavement, the coughing-strangling zombie noise that is right at his feet upon which he cannot focus because of the urgency of the vehicular situation at hand. At the end of this very brief, thoughtful moment, Ludlow wishes he were a better cop. He wishes he could see where Smith was, see if he is OK. And he wishes he were Smith, someone with real potential that he knows, someone who someday might actually do something, dig his way out of the deep ditch of his life. Someone who might stand up, walk over and talk to the girl. And, Ludlow wishes, finally, that the classic automobile was going forward – that is, heading in his direction front-end first, so that if he were to shoot at it, his bullet would hit the engine or some otherwise useful part of it so that it might actually stop. *Ah, if wishes were horses....*

Frustrated, Smith has a burst of strength, rolling the seemingly dead weight off of his back, and props on his knees. He coughs deeply and pukes onto the ground, clearing his pipes of dirt, sand, dust, chewed churro, chimichanga, red rice, refried beans, chopped lettuce and a tall sweet-tea. He carefully gets to his feet, thinking that he is a perfectly good target at this point for whatever madness has expanded out exponentially from this vomitous ground-zero. Time to get to the car and call in backup for a...what? Domestic disturbance?

Then, the holiest of crap. Through his tearing, bleary eyes, he sees Ludlow with his piece drawn, aiming at a...vehicle backing towards him with a whining-roar.

Oh, no. Not again.

But Ludlow doesn't pull the trigger. He dodges to the left, in careful, quick, rather mincing steps and the beautiful (once, long ago) old sports car goes right by – *Ole!* – and crumples the front-right-bumper and quarter panel of the prowler with a sound similar to someone banging on a drum-kit. The big, heavy police car halts the runaway T-Bird dead in its tracks. Ludlow then scampers over to see that the driver is another little old man in his underwear. Is this a thing? Does no one wear pajamas anymore? He reaches in, twists and yanks the keys out of the ignition, anyhow, and keeps his pistol out in his other hand. The world is a strange place, after all, a madhouse, and you just never know how one moment of batshit-crazy might lead to another.

Woodrow leaned back in the cockpit of the T-Bird. His neck hurt. For just a moment, he thought that he was sitting at his desk, in the very comfortable executive chair, doing... work related stuff of the type, variety and frequency of boring that made a weekday slide by so glacially that it must actually affect the space-time continuum enough that he might not getting older. Then the chair hit the back of his head with such force that he was thrown forward against the desk which was really a steering wheel and he depressed the horn-bar and it tooted familiarly so that he was thrust back into the present moment against the will of the various spirits circumnavigating his circulatory system. Then quiet, blessed and yet off-putting. Not moving anymore? Damn.

After giving the man who fell on top of him enough of a glance to ensure that he hasn't suffered some sort of thrombosis-related-activity, (the fellow is staring at the mess Smith deposited on the ground next to him, looking for portents?) Smith coughs and spits his way over to his partner.

"Holy fucking shit," he says. A full notch up in the exclamatory holies.

"Please step out of the car, sir." Ludlow says, keeping his pistol drawn, but not actually pointing it at the driver. Good boy, Smith thinks. We may just yet get out of this alive.

Brushing what foul crud he can off the front of his uniform with his free hand, Smith returns to the man on the ground, who is now up on his bare, bleeding feet, shivering. Asks him if he's OK, gets enough of an affirmative that he is satisfied, and has him hobble over to the curb and sit. The man in the car, led by Ludlow, joins him. Side by side, they make a pathetic, somehow symbiotic, pair, Smith decides, then realizes he's thinking as much about himself and his partner as these two elder...ahem, statesmen.

A new set of lights approach – flickering blue and red. Keifer? Well, there you are. Smith' shoulders slump. His back hurts, he stinks of puke and something else...what did that barefoot old guy play in? At the moment, Ludlow, at least seems professional, but there will still be a story to tell later, and a report to write, and no doubt he'll get that wrong, very wrong. They'll have to reweave the loose ends a bit together.

Smith stands arms akimbo in the oncoming headlights.

Yes, life is short and a lot strange. Tonight, that is, *tomorrow*, and if he still has a job, he is going to go to the Tex-Mex place for dinner and have a chimichanga picadillo and a sweet tea (or maybe a Coke) and while he's there, he is going to walk over to the cash register desk and excuse himself and ask Serena if sometime, maybe when she has a moment free – see, he knows she's busy with school and such – but just maybe she would like to go see a movie with him, or a sunset. Or get a cup of coffee.

Wait. What if Serena isn't her name?

Ludlow and Smith, those nitwits. Did you hear about how they kept the banker and the newspaper editor from killing each other? Wrecked that beautiful '63 Thunderbird, though. Didn't you hear? What a scandal....

Author Bio

Garrison Somers is a writer, editor, reader and observer who lives in Chapel Hill.